The Tower Card

It's the end of your world

Book One
in the Tarot Series

A novel by

John Berry Deakyne

Sedona WordSmith
Sedona, Arizona

The Tower Card

ISBN: 978-0-9830973-0-3

Published by Sedona WordSmith
PO Box 1726, Sedona, Arizona 86339

Library of Congress Cataloging
Deakyne, John Berry / The Tower Card

Cover design by Kerry Bober and *Peace, Love & Art*
http://www.peaceloveandart.com

Printed in the U.S.A.

My deepest gratitude to all the
angels who guided me here,
especially Meredith –
my teacher, my rock,
my Justine.

In memory of Roxanne.

Fore-word to The Tower Card

So, how does it end up that a man raised in the Bible-belt, son of a Baptist preacher and a preacher's daughter ends up writing a novel with the Tarot at its center? My father would not even let us play with standard playing cards because he believed they were birthed from the Tarot; he was right.

But I am not some disillusioned disciple with a grudge against traditional Christianity. I have been in churches all my life. I was the president of the youth group; I preached the sermons on youth Sundays; I taught Sunday school and Bible School into my young adulthood and I knocked on strangers doors and shared with them the "Four Spiritual Laws".

And even in this time when so many of my peers are reluctant to identify themselves as "Christian" because the label is too limiting and suggests archaic and closed-down views of God and the Universe, I claim the brand. I have found redemption for my early religious training in the teachings of the "New Thought" movement and even in the Shamanic tradition which was my entry point into alternative spirituality.

I have studied the Christian scriptures and I do not find them to be at odds with the best of other spiritual teachings. And for all the times he has fallen into disfavor, Yeshua Ben

Yosef (Jesus) rises again as my personal guide, the master of masters, and worthy of my following him.

While others have found the more recent rumors of Jesus being linked with a wife (or even worse, a lover) as besmirching his divine character, I find that portrayal refreshing. From an early age I was able to glean the humanity of the man, Jesus, from between the lines in the gospels, and his association with a powerful feminine force reinforces the call for all awakening beings to embrace the sacred marriage of the divine masculine and the divine feminine as we enter into this new age of existence.

Knowing that Jesus is called "the prophet out of Egypt" by some ancient historians makes an interesting end-run back to the Tarot which many suggest also had its origins in the Egyptian Mystery Schools which were thriving in the Hebrew communities of Egypt where Jesus was raised and trained. Many believe it was Jesus' teaching of these mystery traditions that set him at odds with the church of his day; which threatened the authorities to such a degree that he had to be disposed of. It was and is still a radical teaching that "the kingdom of heaven is within you."

So the Tarot is packed full of images and symbols of the ancient mysteries, both Christian and pre-Christian. Even the symbols of the cross, and the dove, and the fish pre-date the Christian tradition – they were co-opted and incorporated by that new and dangerous religion.

When the Jesus Cult moved out of secret gatherings in living rooms and into churches and cathedrals, the institution of the church came to regard as threatening some of the fringe players in the Jesus movement who sought a more inclusive rather than exclusive practice. Many were calling for a practice grounded in love rather than law. So, the ancient symbols, including many Christian symbols, were embedded in playing cards. The cards were designed to appear harmless and innocent and likely to fly past the noses of the church hierarchy without detection.

The Tarot was used as a parlor game and the symbols rested there as reminders about the Great Mystery that promised to liberate the mind and soothe the soul . . . and possibly to foment a revolution against the conventional ways of looking at spirituality, the conventional ways of being, when the time was right.

Now is our time.

John Berry Deakyne

The Tower Card

PROLOGUE

This is the story, the journey of Adam, who here will move from deep sleep to blessed awakening. He is me – but he is another seeker. Like me, his whole world will need to fall into shambles before he can become his true Self.

It started downtown on the plaza – it was a fundraiser for the town museum. There was a scattering of homemade booths selling baked goods next to the farmer's market. She, Cherie, was busy as usual making the rounds. She would chat up every wealthy person – man or woman – she could spot.

At some point she would laugh and throw back her head full of thick yellow hair, laying her hand softly on the arms of silver-haired gentlemen who would delight at her touch and her attention, cementing her into their memory next time they wanted to buy or sell a house. Or, they would send her their friend from the city who needed a wine country retreat and who expected to be treated with due deference.

She would not surface for hours, and the husband, Adam, would be reduced to amusing himself with looking at fresh Bing cherries and tables of pottery. At one point, when she had completely focused her attention on another, Adam saw his opening and pulled away from her considerable gravity.

He was moving to the center of the plaza when he noticed a small child, a little girl about three years old, looking all around for what must be a missing parent, just on the brink of tears. Adam conducted a quick search of the area looking for any potential owners, and then he squatted down to engage the small being. She was a cherub with beautiful red curls falling over her eyes and onto her red tinted cheeks and she was on the edge of exploding. He said, "Where is your mommy?"

At the word "mommy" she roared with overwhelming fear and desperation. He had kicked open the floodgates and now the tears and wailing poured out. Adam was quite startled by the sudden show of emotion, still squatting, and afraid to touch the poor child, but wanting to comfort her. He held out his arms to her, hoping to lift her to some official table where they would be able to locate the mommy. Suddenly, the mommy was over him, hovering, like a raptor. She swooped in and swept the screaming child into her arms. Mommy quickly transported the tiny being out of reach, glaring at him with eyes full of fury and reproach.

A small crowd had gathered around the spectacle and Adam finally rose to a standing position, the onlookers still gazing at him with suspicion. He brought up both his hands, palms to the sky, and said, "What?"

He escaped the mob before they could gather torches and pitchforks and continued his move to the center of the plaza looking for a refuge. "What's that, a chair?"

2

It was under a soaring live oak in the center of the plaza, seemingly unoccupied beside an abandoned card table. He looked around trying to find the vendor, then he gratefully took a seat.

She came from behind the tree – seeming to apparate – and took the seat facing him. He could not see her clearly because of the dark blue cloak she rested under. He immediately tried to rise, "I'm sorry – I didn't know anybody was here."

She reached out to touch him, holding him to the table; the chair. "Stay here – you are exactly where you belong."

He settled into the chair, starring at the apparition. She pulled out a deck of cards and laying them on the table said, "Shuffle."

Adam protested. "Hey, I was just looking for a place to sit down. I'll pay for the privilege. It's for charity, isn't it? I'm not buying anything."

He could see just the glint of blue eyes under the blue cloak – unusual, exotic for a person with such dark skin. He sensed there was some extraordinary beauty here within his reach, but beyond his grasp.

She said, "You're here, I'm doing readings, and like you said, it's for charity."

He settled into his chair, she set the deck before him, and said again, "Shuffle."

Self-consciously he took the deck. "Like playing cards?"

She nodded yes. "Two more times, then set them out in three piles." He did. "Now pick one."

He hesitated. She said, "Don't think!"

He quickly pointed to the pile on his left. It felt correct. She collected the other two piles and set them aside. She told him, "Take the first card and turn it over."

ZERO – THE FOOL

He turned over the card and saw its number was zero. He saw the image of a carefree, young vagabond nonchalantly stepping off the side of a sheer cliff. At the bottom of the card were the words "The Fool." He curled his forehead and said, "That can't be good."

The woman emerged from her cloak a little further. He saw red painted lips – part of the show, no doubt – and those eyes, still surprising blue against flawless mocha skin and spiraling curls of ebony hair escaping from the hood to frame a gentle face, It's the best card in the deck," she said. "Very lucky.

"He is pure potential. Unless you tell him he can't, he will fly. The whole world is available to you – you may accomplish anything – you may now achieve your heart's desire."

He looked up at her with a sudden smile and a small surge of relief.

Adam wandered dazed around the plaza for some time, thinking he should find his wife – but kept forgetting why. He finally ran into her at the fountain and they made their way to the parking lot, found the Lexus, and headed home to the elite neighborhood, that section to the north of Santa Rosa reserved for the successful and the upwardly mobile.

He didn't speak at all on the way home. He was still a bit rattled from his encounter with the Tarot reader. No matter – Cherie kept up a constant wall of sound, energized by all the potentially lucrative contacts she had made, all the business cards she had handed out to serious future buyers and sellers.

"Really golden prospects." She repeated, "The best people in town were there – they don't come out for everything. Oh, and an invitation to the McMurray Ranch event next week – that is pure gold!"

Adam sat in the passenger seat as she raced the Lexus SUV past vineyards and tidy strip malls. Nice car, though more than they could afford. She could explain it better than he. "An investment … it's all about first impressions ... you have to look successful to be successful ... worth its weight in gold!" He stared at her, hearing nothing – still just a wall of sound. He noticed how pretty she was: perfectly-styled blond hair, fine features, lips still moving – a perfect shade of pink. So unlike the woman in the plaza.

He had been dazzled by Cherie when they first met in college, the University of Colorado in Boulder. She was the sorority stereotype – pretty, of course, active, on committees, already making contacts, not a great student. He was the scholar – excelling in that role, slightly left of center, moving off-campus his sophomore year with an eclectic group of guys in a big old house on "the hill."

They played guitar and talked about starting a band, playing professionally; they were pretty good he thought. They talked politics, religion, philosophy, the environment – unnoticeably sliding to the liberal edge on every important issue, matching the personae of the town they had invaded. Now – like all the others – they planned to never leave.

He was the sage of the house. He waxed poetic over Thoreau and Emerson, avidly promoting the elderly professor who taught the seminar on Transcendentalist Literature. Later, when he and Cherie made their unlikely pairing, she would look at him, dismayed, and say, "I think you are a Transcendentalist," which in her voice sounded more like "I think you are a communist, or an anarchist, a subversive."

He would laugh out loud. "Yeah . . . probably . . . you should come to one of our meetings." Later he would have to explain there were no meetings. How he loved those wide bewildered eyes.

"Doesn't matter," she would say, and then recite a list of tasks that must be accomplished before the spring formal: pick up tux, order flowers, rent a car – his old Honda would never do.

He merely humored her, never guessing that would become his primary profession for the next thirty years.

Now, he wondered what she ever saw in him. He resisted her every push and pull toward civility. She endlessly arranged his hair, his wardrobe, his entourage. He loved his torn and faded jeans – his chosen uniform, all denim and the occasional flannel shirt. Wouldn't she have preferred one who didn't need to be re-dressed, re-trained? There were plenty of those at the debauched frat parties she attended. Plenty of smart-looking, clean cut, neat and tidy, Republican boys, prepackaged, to suit her.

Maybe it was the lure of something slightly sinful, or the challenge of tearing him down and rebuilding him in her image, some sordid science project. He still did not know. Even her father had not approved, the one she admired and worshipped. When she took him to New Hampshire that Easter holiday, to meet the family, the tension had been palpable.

Her father was a self-made man, not college educated, but a voracious reader. She thought her dad was the smartest man alive. Adam expected to meet a saint and was sorely disappointed. What he met was a pompous, grandiose megalomaniac who loved nothing more than hearing himself talk. If Adam had "ooh'd" and "aah'd" over those self-serving stories, he could have ingratiated himself with the old man. But he could not bring himself that low, not then. He observed in Cherie how the power of familial love could veil the truth of the other's shortcomings. He thought that if she met this man on the street, she would find him disgusting.

At that time, he was certain of his own future success in music or film – something creative – and that would soon enough earn him prestige and monetary rewards that would eclipse the shallow success of this poser. Then the beautiful sorority girl would come around to know which of them was truly the better man.

Tonight as he sat beside her, listening to the drone, and still admiring her stately beauty, he could not dredge up any righteous fury. He doubted himself – he could not say he was the better man. His wife certainly made a respectable living, hauling in handsome commissions even in a down economy.

Her father would fawn over her. In a booming voice he would boast, "She could sell ice-cubes to Eskimos."

It was certainly true – and Adam had used the exact quote – when she was out of ear-shot. Adam had bounced around, failing as a musician and a songwriter. Today he never even picked up his guitar. He had a trunk full of songs that nobody wanted.

He transformed his ability to fix things and to figure out how things worked into a job as a facilities manager. He had a crew, he hired and fired, and he trained people, but he felt like a glorified handyman. He kept a job he hated and worked for a man who demeaned him. He brought home a modest paycheck that paid the mortgage and most of the bills. The bulk of his wife's income went toward buying the things to keep up the façade of an upper middle class household and the impression that they would not hesitate to procure anything they desired.

Cherie was always on the verge of some big deal; the one last deal that would land them on easy street. Their success was always around the corner and he had stopped anticipating, stopped believing the lie. The fortune teller had not read his future – she assured him she was reading his present and what she saw had startled him. In his mind he knew he was on a new path – he did not know what it was or where it led, and he did not too much care.

When Cherie pulled the car into the drive, their ten-year-old dog, Badger, jumped at the front gate, moaning and yelping like he had been abandoned for days or weeks. It was his dog – he had found him at a rescue shelter when he was just a puppy. But Badger immediately bonded with Cherie, maybe because she was trying to remain aloof and indifferent about the dog. Adam had worked on his wife for months leading up to the adoption; she was largely against extending the family, but finally relented. Adam had grown up with multiple animals in the household and longed for a trusted animal companion. And though he fed the dog, took him to the vet, cared for his every need, at the end of the day, Badger would curl up next to wherever Cherie had landed.

Cherie had preferred to give the dog a more stately name but the shelter had named him Badger because of the wide strip of white down his longish snout. The rest of him was a reddish brown and they could never name entirely all the breeds he represented – terrier, pointer, cow-dog, even some greyhound. He was the smartest dog Adam had ever seen – somewhat indifferent about human contact, good with kids, and very defensive about protecting Cherie from any other dog. When she would walk Badger in the neighborhood, other walkers would want to steer their friendly dogs toward them to have a sniff.

Cherie would unapologetically tell them to stay away, warning "He's not friendly." The dog would unknowingly protect her from engaging the neighborhood which would have also caused her to break her brisk stride and aerobic rhythm.

Adam fed the dog and freshened the water dish. When they arrived in the kitchen, the wall of sound was still roaring. At the counter she unloaded her woven bag. She said "Look, Sun Gold tomatoes – the first of the season. Salad tomorrow."

She set the small golden orbs in the sink and continued, "My God, what a night. I'm just floating; and a million things to do."

She finally noticed his melancholy silence, "Are you listening to me?"

Adam was suddenly pulled back into the room, "Uh . . . well . . . no. I was just thinking."

Cherie replied with distaste, "Thinking? What are you thinking about?"

"I am wondering why people are so unhappy . . . when they could be happy . . . by just changing their mind. I'm wondering why we can't be happy."

She defended, "What in the hell are you talking about? Haven't you been listening to me? I am happy. I had a great night. This is me . . . happy. I don't know when I've been this happy."

Adam tried to explain. The thoughts were just taking shape in his head and he could not quite give them a convincing form. "I'm talking about on the inside. That's where I'm not happy. I'd like to change that."

Cherie was not ready for this seriousness. "I don't know what you've been smoking, but you need to get a grip." She busied herself with putting the house to bed, and Adam sank back into himself.

He managed to change the subject. "Hey, do you know that lady that was giving readings in the park?"

His wife looked at him like he was drooling. He tried to elaborate. "The tarot reader, under the tree, she was dark

11

skinned with blue eyes – very pretty. She gave me a reading. She was quite serious . . . and a little scary."

Cherie continued looking at him without an answer until he gave up. She noticed the surrender, saying, "Good, I'm going to bed. Don't forget to call the gardener tomorrow. They've got to dig out that patch by the patio."

Adam was almost always in bed before her, because she had a complex regimen every night that preserved her smooth skin; that warded off the threat of dark circles and creases. Tonight he was sitting up with a book when she emerged from the bathroom, rubbing lotion on her arms. Adam set down his book to watch her move across the room. She was his wife. After thirty years he thought he should know her better, but tonight he had a sense that there was something hidden, something unknowable about her that he could not penetrate.

She finally noticed him watching, saying, "What?"

He answered, "Nothing. I was just noticing how pretty you are."

Cherie was surprised by this unexpected observation. "Really? Isn't that sweet?" She leaned across the bed and gave him a quick peck on the lips, then promptly returned to her region of the bed, readying herself for slumber.

When she reached to turn off the bed-side lamp, Cherie noticed that Adam was still looking at her like he wanted to ask a question. She said, "Don't even think about it. I'm exhausted. And you've got to get up early. Turn off your light. You know I can't sleep with that on."

Adam switched off his light and sat there in the darkness while Cherie settled herself into the system of pillows, her back to the husband. In the dim, with just a faint glow filtering through the drapes from some distant street light, he reached out and set his hand on Cherie's shoulder. She did not move or say a word. He let it stay there a few moments – then he pulled back and lay down. Adam studied the ceiling for some time, eyes wide open.

ONE – THE MIND

He turned over the next card and was confronted with a monster. The card was titled "Mind" and the imperturbable reader's face took on the slightest frown. There was a monstrous dark face holding a jumble of hard machinery, a grotesque mouth and smokestacks protruding from the top of the head.

He looked to her for guidance and she shook her head, saying, "This should be very familiar to you. It's a mirror."

He wanted to say, "You don't know me." But he held back – maybe she did know him. The thought was disturbing, but behind that was the thought that somebody understood what he was going through. A stranger. Someone he would never see again.

She said, "Your mind thinks it's a real person. It keeps you from understanding and acting on what your heart knows now and has known forever. The mind is NOT your enemy – it is your servant – and must never be your master. It will sabotage your peace if you let it."

Adam thought, "What peace?"

"You cannot stop the intrusion of the mind by effort. You actually have to stop trying, and just let it fall away. When you remove the voices and blocks, what is left is who you really are. Peel away the layers. At the bottom you will find what you have always known to be true: you are connected to that truth through the heart and not mind. Let it all fall away – you will lose nothing – and you just might find the secret.

Adam had to ask, "The secret?"
She answered, "The reason you were born."

At work the next day, Adam went through the motions.
This time he had landed at a time-share property that was filled
every weekend with folks too poor to buy something at the
Hyatt or the Wyndham. He moved his crew out to make repairs
and clean the grounds; to turn over the just-emptied condos.
He got himself a cup of coffee, closed the door to his office,
and turned on a little soft music. He wanted to revisit his
encounter with the tarot reader, and maybe even plan his next
move. Sooner or later he would have to face the reality that
was Phil, the resort manager, his boss.

The good part was that although Phil was an obsessive
workaholic, he liked to come in around nine or so. Adam, who
arrived at seven, usually had two glorious hours to himself.

But not today. Phil tore open his office door without any
niceties, "Why the hell you got your door closed?! You know
we got an open door policy around here!" Phil required
everyone's door be open except his own. Evidently he had
super secret executive tasks that no one should be privy to.

He could not stop. "Have you seen the parking lot?! It
looks like hell! No, I mean it literally looks like hell."

Adam managed a response, "I guess you would literally
know."

"Is that a joke? Is that your idea of joke? You need to get
someone out there before someone complains. I swear – if
someone complains, your job is on the line."

Instead of fighting him, Adam was set to go out to assess the damage and to pick it up himself. He did not want to drag one of his guys away from their work. He said, "I'll do it myself."

"Oh my God, you're serious. Why do you think we hire those uneducated, completely unskilled Mexicans? So you can go out there with your college education and pick up trash? No wonder you can't get anything done!"

Adam got on the talkie, "José, I need you to meet me in the parking lot with a garbage bag. You got two minutes."

The talkie responded, "Roger."

On his way out, Adam got in his retort, "You know – firing me would be like Christmas in July. Put me out of my fucking misery. Seriously."

Phil was ready, "No damn way, dude – I'm keeping you around just to make your life a living hell."

Adam had one more. "Get in line."

The rest of the day, Adam went through the motions. He knew he did a half-assed job. His own crew picked up the vibe, and did the bare minimum, and that didn't bother him one bit. His whole day was an exercise in figuring out how to get by with the least amount of effort, the least distress, and his crew appreciated his hands off approach. In their own way they were loyal.

He could not give himself entirely to this effort or even to the guys who worked for him. Some of them barely spoke English and, with his limited use of Spanish, they managed to do what they were hired to do. The workers spoke among themselves and Adam often felt apart, detached. He saw them clearly, empathized, and maybe even loved them.

He knew most of them had lived already with some hardness. Some had made their way from Mexico or further south and had managed at least to get the papers that allowed this enterprise to hire them. Some were born here but still lived in the exclusively Latino barrio at the south edge of town. Some had gang affiliations. All had tattoos that bragged about their heritage and their associations. He had all these thoughts and feelings, but he could not help them – he could not help himself.

Shortly after their lunch break he got a call from his crew, "Come quick! It's Antonio – he's bleeding!"

Adam did not hesitate. He took off on foot across the lawn to the shop, Phil trailing right behind. He knew Phil would be instantly obsessed with thoughts of liability. They found Antonio surrounded by the crew – a bloody gash on his forehead – and the crew leader, José, applying pressure. Adam grabbed the first aid kit and quickly applied a sterile pad to the wound – told José to keep up the pressure. He quickly got the report: Antonio had turned around quickly in the pool pump room and cracked his head on a low hanging pipe.

Adam kept his cool and got the guys to escort the victim to his pickup. Phil looked at him with concern, worry in his eyes. Adam was in no mood to make his boss feel safe. He said, "Call the ER – tell them we're coming – head gash – going to need stitches."

Phil was worried about a lawsuit, "Are you sure? Stitches?"

Adam yelled at him as he ran to the truck, "Just make the call!"

Antonio held the compress to his head while Adam raced the few miles north to the small hospital. Adam was not really worried – he knew that head wounds bled a lot. Antonio would take a couple stitches, have a headache, and be just fine. Adam waited in the lobby while they treated his man. He had some time to think, to clear his head. He knew he could have had anyone else take this man to the hospital. It was a menial task, really – just driving and then waiting. To him it was more like a sacred duty. He was responsible for his workers – and if one of them bled, he bled for the boss. Yes, it was just an accident, they happen every day. He couldn't even explain it to himself – he just knew it had to be him.

They released Antonio from the emergency room, and Adam dropped him off at his home in South Santa Rosa before he headed north to the "better" side of town. The crewman's wife came out of the house in an apron – full of concern and a stream of questions. Antonio, slightly embarrassed, introduced his wife, but she rightly had no time – and no concern for this other man. Adam left his man in the heart of his family where he would surely rest and heal.

Somehow this incident made Adam more certain of his own intention. On his way home he was determined to have it out with Cherie. He would make her stop the chatter – he would force her to come down to something real, to stop, to

18

shut up, and to listen. Still, he had no idea what he would say –
he thought if they had a moment of honesty between them the
words might manifest themselves, something holy might arise.

Adam imagined that he and his wife, his true one, had
once been madly in love. He remembered the long
conversations that lasted long into the night – discussions
where they had mapped out a future full of adventure, and
discovery, and love. Love – what the hell happened to love?
Today it felt like something cold and lonely. For God's sake,
how can you feel lonely when you are constantly with
someone? Hadn't they loved each other once? Hadn't they
longed for each other – and delighted at each other's touch?

It seemed so long ago, a memory, a fantasy: lying together
in his bed at school under cool sheets, sinking into the
afterglow of freshly made love. When he was in her, when
their passion was at its peak, there was abandon there. No
posturing, no filling the air with meaningless banter. There
was something real. He felt he had touched the face of God
when he touched her face – like he had kissed God right on the
lips when he kissed her lips. They were close to something
there – or was it only him? It felt true. He wondered if they
could find that thing again. It had been such a long time since
they had felt anything true, anything like passion.

The loneliest part of his day now was lying down with his
wife at night. She loved their big king bed with the high-thread
count sheets and the Italian fabric pillows. She loved that big
bed were they could lie together and never know the other was
also there, each carving out their own space. He knew she was

19

only inches away but it felt like miles. It wasn't the sex he missed – it was the affection, the intimacy beneath the sex, the love – something that went beyond infatuation, beyond desire and want, something that lifted them both. It felt so far away and he wondered if it had ever been real.

Cherie's busy-ness kept them from connecting physically. She always seemed so far away. And she had always been very particular about coupling. Everything had to be perfect. The time had to be right. She had to be fully rested and not distracted. Sometimes an occasion, like his birthday, would create an opening; Easter might provide a moment – certainly not Good Friday. But even then, the intimacy felt forced, obligatory, insincere, empty. He almost dreaded those occasions now, because he also had to pretend – to play his part.

Adam would need a little more courage before he faced his wife so he headed to the Corner Bar to see if he could locate his friend. He found Bud on his usual stool and plopped down next to him, ordering a pint of the local brew. Bud joked, "Hey, what's the occasion? Somebody die?"

Adam took a long pull on his beer, "No, but I'm going to kill my boss."

Bud was resourceful. "You need help with the boss? I know some great ways to dispose of a body."

Adam let it out. "I wish it was just the boss. My life sucks!"

Bud tried to quiet him down. "Take it easy, man. If I was doing your wife, I'd be the happiest man in town."

Adam confessed, "Yeah, I might be too, if I was doing my wife."

"Ouch, that hurts. Most guys won't admit it." Bud tried to change the subject. "Hey I saw you at the fundraiser. You were all spaced out."

"What do you mean?"

"Under the old oak tree, you were talking to yourself. I was going to stop and help you find your medication, but I was late to meet my girl."

Adam was brought back to earth. "Right, under the big oak, it was amazing. Then you saw her, the tarot reader. That really pretty black woman with blue eyes. Who in the hell is she?"

Bud looked at his friend with concern. "There was no woman, dude. You're losing it."

"You were drunk. I can't believe you didn't see her. You wouldn't forget. That reading changed me. I had an epiphany."

Bud shook his head. "What are you going to do?"

"I'm going to change my life, one step at a time. I might quit my job. Oh, and I'm getting a little brother. The Big Brothers program – I already got matched. I always wanted kids."

"You're kidding me. Your wife won't give you kids so you go out and get one on your own. What'd Cherie say?"

"She doesn't know yet. I'm telling her tonight, and meeting the kid tomorrow."

Bud summed it up. "Man, you are over your head."

Adam had more. "And I've got to talk to a social worker. It's serious; the kid is some kind of special case."

"The wife is going to kill you."

Adam thought his friend was probably right. "I'm going to need another beer."

When Cherie pulled the Lexus into the garage Adam was deep in thought. She ran into the house offering a cursory greeting to the dog, none to him. She was rattling as usual, set down her designer briefcase, and took off her designer blazer. He caught her in the kitchen, between the granite island and the stainless cook-top. "Cherie, we need to talk."

Surprised, she said, "We are talking."

"No, we really need to talk. I'm drowning here. I told you, I'm not happy."

"What do you have to be unhappy about? Look around. We have a beautiful house."

He was shoved off topic. "We're upside down on the mortgage – we owe more than own."

"Daddy says it's good debt; an investment."

"What about us? What's going on with us? We don't talk – not really."

"We talk constantly. What's wrong with you – one of those mid-life things again?"

"We used to talk about having a family – about doing things – what happened to those kids?"

"They grew up and got jobs and a mortgage. Listen, Adam, it's going to get better – I'm just so busy at work. After we get this project launched, after we drop the mail – I'll have time for you. After we get the landscaping done in the backyard I'll be able to focus. I just can't concentrate when everything is undone – you know that. It wouldn't hurt if you gave me hand with the garden – that gardener is not doing a good job. You need to call him – I gave you the number – tell me you called him today."

Adam just stopped and looked at her. She said, "What?"

"Can't we just be real? God-damn-it, I miss you. I want to feel close to you – like we used to."

He moved to her, to embrace her, but she recoiled. "I don't have time for this. Just get a grip – if you want sex just say so. I'll try to pencil you in."

Hurt, he knew how to get her to focus. "I think I'll quit my job."

He got her attention. "You can't quit your job – don't even think about it – I cannot support the two of us. And I will not go to my dad again for money – it's humiliating."

He was pleading now. "I hate it. I'm filled with dread from the moment I wake up in the morning till I go to bed at night – then I dream of toilets overflowing and Phil yelling about trash in parking lot."

"You need to sit that little bastard down and set him straight. You don't know how to deal with people in authority. They have to be managed. I have a book – where is it? You have to read this book."

She rummaged in her desk and Adam grasped for something to land on. "Maybe we should have a kid. We talked about having kids."

"Jesus, let's just buy a Volkswagen van and move to Timbuktu. Have you lost your mind?" Then, changing the subject, quickly, "If you quit your job, what would you do? You just said we've got debt up to our eyeballs."

"Thought I might go back to school – maybe get my teacher's certificate. If I can't be a rock-star, maybe I can teach music."

"Don't you know that's the first thing they cut? They are firing music teachers, not hiring. You have to consider the market. Besides, we don't have time for that right now. Wait till we get on our feet."

Adam was exasperated. "We are always waiting for something to happen before we can be happy. Why can't we be happy now? You know there is only Now! Now is all we have. There's no later on. There's no tomorrow."

Cherie came down a notch to console him. "Honey, we have to be realistic. I know you want to live on a cloud – so do I. But, for now we have to be in the real world. This is where we live. We have to make the best of it."

"Is that what we're doing?"

"Now, that is just mean."

"I'm serious. Those Mexican guys that work for me living paycheck to paycheck have a better life than I do. Yes, they hate their jobs, but when they go home their kids come running out to hug their daddy. Their tired wives in their dirty aprons and Wal-Mart dresses are happy that daddy's home. There's laughing and music and tenderness."

"And that's what you want?'

"That's exactly what I want."

She was done with this. "Then you married the wrong chick."

They faced each other in silence, a fatal resentment filling up the space between. Adam had almost forgotten to tell her the news.

He spoke calmly. "I'm going to change my life; you don't have to help. I'm taking it one step at a time. I'm volunteering with the Big Brothers program, already signed all the papers, got screened, fingerprinted, background check. They matched me right away; some kid they want to pair up right away. I'm meeting him tomorrow and then some social worker."

She was frustrated that he could not see the plain truth. "This is your plan? You don't have time for this. And I certainly don't. . . ."

He interrupted, "You don't have to do a damn thing. It's just me and him. And I'm not asking permission. You might see him around the house – at least say 'hi', or wave."

"If you think your life is so bad, I don't know why you want to pull a troubled kid into it. At least lock up the silver. You don't know what kinds of homes these kids come out of." Cherie was finished with this. She washed her hands and moved to a neutral corner of the house.

That night, before Cherie got up from her computer and readied for bed, Adam moved some fresh bedding and a change of clothes into the guest room. He made the smaller queen bed, changed into a t-shirt and gym shorts, and sat up in bed with a book. He left the door open so that Cherie knew she could come in if she wanted to talk. He heard her walk down the hallway and enter their bedroom.

After some time, she closed the door to their bedroom, like she did every night – shutting out the rest of world so she could enter her sleep cycles without interruption. This time, when she shut out the rest of the world, she shut him out.

TWO – TOTALITY

She told him to turn over the next card; he did. It read "Totality". He saw acrobats, like in a circus, swinging from two trapeze toward each other, one performer on each swing, holding on with their knees – between them a third acrobat with long hair being thrown from one pair of hands (releasing) to another pair (receiving). The dark woman said, "This is you in the middle. But if you don't give yourself to this, you'll fall and die. That's the totality: you must give yourself to this entirely or the next experience, the one that's waiting for you, cannot receive you."

Adam looked up from the card. "What am I releasing? And, what is receiving me?"

He wasn't exactly what Adam expected. He looked to be about twelve, maybe thirteen – awkward age – already feeling a contraction in his gut. Jesus, this kid is trouble – wouldn't be in the program if he wasn't. Okay, what did the reader say? "Be fearless."

The boy was just getting out of school for the day, meeting this strange man at the juice bar next door. He reached out his hand. "I'm Adam. You must be Leo."

Leo shrugged a hello and held out his hand – no grip at all, no confidence, no sense of self. "Leo, that's a great name, the lion, very cool."

Leo shrugged again. Adam went to the counter and got them each a beverage. The high school kid behind the counter made them some fruit smoothies. He guessed on what the kid would like – the sweeter the better, plenty of orange sherbet. He returned with the drinks, Leo took his sullenly, and pulled on the straw. They sat in strained silence with occasional forced talking, sipping on their drinks, Adam trying to see his eyes, Leo avoiding the other's gaze. He was African American with a short cropped 'fro – unusual enough – not too many black folk north of the city. How typical, Adam thought, that the ethnic kids get dumped into these programs.

Adam tried to break the ice. "I'm new at this, so you're going to have to take it easy on me. I just thought we could spend some time together – hang out. It'd be good for both of us. I don't mind the company."

Leo was still focused on his drink. "I guess."

"So, how are you with tools?

Leo answered with a question: "Like, with a hammer?"

"Yeah, I've got a project I need to get started – thought you might like to help. Keep us both busy: me out of my wife's hair; you out of your mom's hair."

Leo finally put more than four words together. "Ain't with my mom - she's in jail. They stuck me in another foster home. Sucks, I'd be better off on my own."

"Jesus, I'm sorry. They didn't tell me. Why's your mom in jail?"

"I don't know – drugs – something with drugs – buying, selling, using – she's fucked up."

Leo waited for some reaction to the profanity. Adam responded without flinching, "Whole things fucked up – I'm so sorry, kid."

Leo said, "I don't think you're supposed to swear."

"Really, Jesus, I didn't know. I'm not much for staying inside the lines."

Leo waited for the thought to take form. "You ain't no pervert, are you?"

Adam laughed hard. "No – I ain't no pervert."

"Okay then, what's the project?"

Adam laid it out for him. Years ago Cherie had bought a vintage 1970 Airstream. This was her solution to the problem of camping. He had always tried to drag her out into the woods to set up a tent and sleep on the ground, to cook over a campfire. It was not her style – "I don't camp." But he loved it and she wanted to humor him then, to accommodate him, but modify the experience enough for her delicate sensibilities. Maybe it would be fun after all. Pull into a full service park next to some woods; get a full hookup, modest little bathroom – no going in the woods, which had mortified her.

The outside of the Airstream had once been restored but the inside was vintage, which meant it had to be gutted and rebuilt. Cherie had seen a photo spread of the exact model trailer sitting in Ralph Lauren's back yard, serving as a guest cottage. She anticipated showing her guests the duplicate experience – Lauren fabric and patterns on the beds, the windows, the walls. Adam assured her that he could do the remodel, save more than a few bucks over time, and with the redo, the thing would appreciate – at least double in value.

But the trailer sat in its storage spot in an open field on the edge of town, weeds growing up around its wheels, ants climbing into the cabinets, waiting. Adam would do the work. He knew the guy who owned the lot and already had permission to run a line to power the tools. He had the plans scribbled into a notebook and this kid – this Leo, this Lion – would work beside him. Adam promised there was a camping trip in his future once the work was done and this seemed to animate the kid. Maybe they would run up to the redwoods or maybe desert – did he like fishing? He was all in.

Adam hesitated to drop in on him again, but Bud was really his only friend in the area, and he had one more thing to run past him. He never went to him for advice, but somehow the visits always made him feel better. As an independent contractor, Bud kept a shop next to his house on a hill just at the edge of town. Adam parked at the bottom of the hill, on the street, and took the steep walk up. He knew his friend would be in the shop, the crew sent home for the day. He would catch him just before his daily pilgrimage to the Corner Bar.

By the time he reached the top of the drive, Adam was huffing. "Jesus, I've got to get in shape."

Bud was blowing sawdust off a portable table saw. "You could have driven up."

"I know – I need the exercise."

"Makes me think of the young bull looking at the cows in the valley – he says, 'Let's run down there and screw one of those cows.' The old bull says, 'Let's walk down there and screw-em-all.'"

It was an old joke but Adam laughed politely. "I'm thinking of getting the band back together."

Bud put down his work. "Now you're talking, brother. Where'd this come from?"

"I'm figuring it out step by step. And, I need to get out of the house."

Bud was sympathetic, "More trouble with the Missus?"

"It's complicated. Cherie's got a lot of good in her – I don't know anybody more generous. She's just so driven – like she's afraid to wake up. Sometimes I just want to grab her and shake her."

"It's getting heavy in here – you need a beer."

Bud went to the shop fridge and pulled out two Heinekens. "This'll help."

"It will help – it just won't be enough."

Bud took a long pull on his beer. "Man, you're being a downer. Look at me – I'm one year out from my divorce and I've never been happier. I hate to say it, but you need to get laid. The day I signed my divorce papers – that night – I went to a party. I was dancing with this woman I never saw before – and that night. . . . Well, I don't kiss and tell. No, that ain't true. I'll tell you anything. What do you want to know?"

"I've heard enough. I've already got images in my mind I think will never come out."

Adam's mood was lightened by this dissertation. Bud continued, "Hey, I'll be your mentor. First of all, if things don't work out with you and Cherie, you don't mind if I check her out – you don't mind, do you?"

"I don't mind – it might help – you know, give her a jump start."

Bud liked the idea, laughing. "Hey, anything for a friend – you know what I mean?"

He continued, "You gotta stick with me dude. I've got this bachelor thing figured out. Don't get me wrong - I love women. But being on my own has opened my eyes – I'm never going back. I mean I've got women – well one, anyway – and sometimes she gets starry-eyed and it's tricky to have to set her straight without chasing her off. You know how many single fifty-something's there are out there – not to mention forty-something's? You could go there. Why the hell not?"

Adam was confused. "Jesus, man, it sounds like you're telling me to get divorced – we're not even there yet. Don't people do things – go to counseling, trial separations – aren't there steps to this? It doesn't sound right to just cut it off."

"It's like a Band-Aid. You want to jerk it off and be done? Or do you want to pull it off real slow, ripping out one tiny hair at a time? Me and the Missus, we went to counseling – big waste of time. Turned into a 'he said, she said.' The worst thing ever. And don't do this: we had a male counselor. I swear to God, he was hitting on her. She was in hog heaven – long suffering wife, Neanderthal husband – I could not win.

And, of course you know how it came out. Take advice from an expert: rip it right off."

Adam wanted to change the subject. I met the little brother today, he's cool.

Bud sneered, "Can you get out of it? You really want to pull a kid into this mess?"

"That's pretty much what Cherie said." He worried over the situation for a moment. "But, you know, it feels just right, even if I got into this for all the wrong reasons. Kids going to help me fix up the Airstream, we're going camping, and I thought he could sit in with the band."

"No way! What about all the drinking, and the swearing, and the dirty jokes? He'll ruin it for all of us!" Bud was exasperated.

Adam defended, "It will be good for all of us. You'll see, you'll like him.

"I'll bet he doesn't even play an instrument. What are you going to have him do, roadie for us?"

Adam was figuring it out. "That might work. I thought he could keep the beat on a hand drum. You know, add some percussion. He's too smart to be a bass player."

Bud was resigning himself to the situation. "Funny. I'll dust off my bass. Yes, I play the bass guitar. We can practice in the garage. I've got lots of room since the Missus moved out."

Adam began, "Okay, we all need practice – just get together and jam, pull out some old songs, maybe some blues.

I've got a trunk full of songs I wrote back in the day. Not so bad I think."

"Sure sounds great. We'll do your songs – dust them off. Who knows, maybe we can get some gigs down at the tavern.

"Let's take small steps, okay? Just get loosened up. Start practicing and we'll see how it goes.

THREE – EXPERIENCING

The next card gave him some ease. It read, "Experiencing". There was a woman in a cloak not unlike the reader, though now she made him think of the Madonna. She was clothed in a golden robe over multi-colored inner garments. There was a pattern of golden leaves laid over the cloak that matched the autumnal leaves on the young tree she held in her arms as if it was a person. Her head was turned and tilted down as if she was listening for a secret message.

The reader's lips curled softly into the slightest smile. "Life is coming to you even if it is undeserved. You will experience the mystery and the gentleness of life, but it will take a form you never expected. You should be prepared to be surprised, no, startled by God. What She has to say is loving and kind, though it may be disruptive to what your mind – you remember him – what your mind imagines to be true."

Back at the house Adam reported on his visit with the wounded lion and their plan to fix up the Airstream. Cherie listened without speaking – feeling out this development, trying not to provide a commentary. He told her how a camping trip would work wonders with this troubled kid. Further, maybe the trailer would be a needed boost to their own circumstance. Maybe they could go off together without any cell phones or fax machines and become reacquainted.

She looked at him with unaccustomed silence. He had a nagging feeling that she didn't want to know him better – or if she really became acquainted with his heart, she might not like what she found. The conversation lagged. There was something about a pending sale she had a piece of. He made small talk about the latest drama at work. They stepped away from each other and again retired to separate corners.

The next meeting with Leo went better. They went out to the storage lot and opened up the Airstream. It was a mess, but Leo thought it was so cool. No doubt he saw his salvation in this tiny house on wheels. Pull it anywhere and you are still at home. It was an enclosure, like a Hobbit's house. Maybe he could crawl inside and be safe and stay inside forever. They had cleaning supplies and a broom – even a Shop-Vac hooked up to the cord that stretched to the caretaker's house.

When Adam pried open the entry door, something unseen scurried to the back of the trailer. Leo asked, "What do you think that was?"

"I don't know. Maybe we'll need some traps."

Leo let his mentor lead the way, commenting, "You're gonna need some big traps."

As they settled into cleaning the trailer inside and out, there was very little speaking – very little to say. They just worked, accumulating dust on their sweaty foreheads and arms.

When they stopped and sat in the shade they were both ready for a Coke and some rest, Adam started, "Feels good to work, doesn't it?"

Leo grunted his agreement, then said, "What would happen if we just took off and drove and never looked back?"

"Well, if we went today, we probably wouldn't make it to Cloverdale. Why do you want to leave?"

"Ain't nothing for me here."

Adam didn't want to waste this opening. "Aren't you afraid of the unknown . . . whatever might be out there just waiting for you to come along?"

"Hell no! I'm afraid of what I know – what I know is here, now. Ain't nothing out there that's worse."

"You know what they say: 'Better the devil you know, than the devil you don't.'"

"If they say that, they are just bonehead stupid."

It made Adam stop because he knew the kid was right. Leo was less afraid of striking out on faith than he was. What was he so afraid of leaving behind? It sure wasn't the job he hated. It wasn't the house that owned him. Was it Cherie? He could not bear the thought of being alone. Alone? He felt alone all the time. He felt alone when she slept next to him. But the alternative at this moment was unimaginable.

The choice today was to live the life in front of him. He loved this wise little kid who didn't know he was gifted. It would do no good to tell him. He rightfully disbelieved everything told to him by adults. He would keep that to himself but treat the small being with the respect and deference that was due to one of royal rank.

Tomorrow he was off to see the social worker – not someone who worked with Leo, but the one who worked with his incarcerated mother, Celeste. It was at the social worker's request, and he was quite unsure as to why. It seemed to him

37

the best course would be to keep them as far apart from each other as possible. Leo hated the foster home, but it was worlds superior to being with his mom.

Once inside the Social Services department, Adam briefly waited in the stark lobby, and then was instructed to find his way back through a maze of cubicles, to look for her name on the outside, the name Justine Robinson. He found the indistinct office space littered with small stacks of paper. She sensed his arrival though her back was to him as she rummaged in a file cabinet; she told him to find a seat.

She was called a Client Advocate and she was lucky enough to have drawn the card that was this poor excuse for anything, Leo's mother. This advocate – whatever she was – was no doubt looking out for the best interests of the mother. Probably thought the kid would ground her, give her life some meaning, some excuse to stay sober, no thought for the kid. To Adam, she was the enemy. He would stand guard. He would be Leo's advocate.

"I know it's here somewhere."

She found the folder and turned to face him. She had a smile full of perfect teeth that disarmed him for a moment. But what took him completely out of his head were the eyes. They were partially obscured behind rectangular glasses with clear frames, and still they seemed to enter what he took to be his soul and started rearranging the furniture. She was saying something but he could not hear the words. He responded with an instinctual nod.

There was something else in those eyes. Something he could not name; something ancient and newborn; some mystery or tragedy or secret knowing. Adam was getting pieces of sentences while thinking, "Those eyes." Dark, but not sinister, he could not see the burnt brown around the pupil; only blackness that went on forever; a bottomless well that seemed to ask him to jump in, a portal to something hidden and wonderful, he only needed to open the door.

She was quite striking – he thought dazzling, probably older than him but it was hard for him to judge such things as he aged. There was a knowing in that face – someone who had lived life and held life in her hands. Not a perfect face – the years had left their imprint – but he could sit here and look upon it all day.

She turned back to the file cabinet behind her, averted her eyes, her smile, and the spell was broken. After that, she seemed to avoid direct eye contact, like she had already driven him to the core; she had sized him up, she had seen enough. There was no resistance left in him. He waited for the next wave.

Adam sat in uncharacteristic silence as she ran down some of the details of the case: Celeste in jail again – petty crime – simple possession – not a serious charge but she was a multiple offender. She would probably get out within the month.

She surprised Adam by speaking honestly. "They'll want to give Leo back to her. They'll say it's to keep families together. Truth is the courts just like to keep all their problems grouped together – everything in one basket. They figure they'll be dealing with Leo in the courts till he dies, so why not speed things up. I'm looking out for the best interest of Celeste, but she's got no business trying to raise a kid. Leo's not my responsibility, but that's not the issue. I talked to the foster parents – they're okay. They are at least smart enough to tell me they think you are this kid's best bet. What do you think?"

He was dismayed at the thought of having to speak, but managed, "I don't know. I just spend time with him. I like him. I don't know what in the hell I'm doing."

"That's not what they say. They say he's been almost no trouble after first threatening to run away."

"Where would he go?"

"These kids end up on the street – often as not. That would be an easy transition for him. What do you talk about?"

"I swear I don't know. Whatever comes up. Sometimes we just sit – we're working on a project. Truth is – he helps me more than I help him. Even tells me when I screw up."

"You know, most of these volunteers see their "little's" only a couple times a month."

"Oh jeez, have they complained? I've seen him three times in the first week. I know there are guidelines – I can scale back. He already asked me if I was a pervert – what must they think?"

Justine laughed out loud, showing all those teeth. "Settle down, Sport. Everybody is saying you're the best thing for him. He can't get too much of this. We just want you to keep it up. A let-down might do damage."

Adam pondered this. "You don't think I'd let him down."

"You just told me you don't know what you're doing. It might seem like a small thing – we just don't want you to stop. Sometimes a person changes their priorities. Life gets in the way of good intentions."

A little bit insulted, Adam replied, "I wouldn't do that. I'm not that guy."

"I'm not trying to scare you. This kid doesn't have much going for him – you might be the one thing that keeps him from sinking."

Adam had to take it in. "This isn't really what I signed up for. I'll do what I can. I can spend time with him – if you want more than that, I don't know. . . ."

"That's all we want. That's all I want. But it's not a small thing – I wanted you to know that. So you don't see anything coming up that would alter what you're doing now? Where does your wife figure into this – you're married, aren't you?"

He didn't want to admit it to her. "Yes. But she's not part of the match. He's seen her maybe once, but it's just me and him. We'll mostly be spending time away from home."

Then, as if he had just gotten the idea, "We're going to go camping!"

Justine smiled at his enthusiasm. "That sounds good. I bring up your wife because it would no doubt be a good thing for Leo to be exposed to women that were not addicts and hustlers – not to mention being witness to a healthy marital relationship. He's probably never seen that."

Adams said unconvincingly, "Yes."

"Is everything okay at home? I know it's none of my business. It's just – well, Leo has had all the exposure to dysfunction that he needs. What am I saying – we're all a little dysfunctional, aren't we?" She laughed laying a hand on his arm – he was speechless again.

"It's a matter of degrees – isn't it? I'm sure there's nothing you could do to hurt him – with the exception of stopping what you're doing. I get a good vibe from you, Adam. I think you might be one of the good ones."

She had him again in the high beams and he could not break the spell. She was nodding and smiling and he knew, waiting for him to say something.

He stuttered, "Well okay – then – we'll just move ahead – working on the trailer – and stuff."

She stood to walk him past the cubicles to the department entrance. He was only conscious of his own stupidity, and did not doubt that he was foaming at the mouth as she took her leave of him, and bid him a pleasant farewell – probably.

When she left him at the stairwell, Adam unconsciously stared after her as she walked back to her cubicle. About halfway down the corridor Justine glanced around and saw him gawking at her. She smiled and raised her hand, waving goodbye. He weakly lifted his hand in response, mortified that she had caught him watching her.

Adam felt the blood rush to his head and neck as he took on a crimson hue.

He stumbled down the stairs to the street, suddenly noticing the business card in his hand and what looked like a hand-written phone number at the bottom.

FOUR – ICE-OLATION

Okay now, another scary one – "Ice-Olation" – with a mournful blue face emerging from a wall of ice rolling out a torrent of yellow tears. Adam looked at the reader, dismayed.

Sensing his despair, she reached for him with her voice. "You feel like you are alone, but at the depth of that feeling is your connection to the one true spirit that is us all. Being one, you never have to feel alone. If solitude is something you fear, the call is to not deny it, but to go toward it, embrace it. You don't want to do this, but this is the key to your salvation. I can tell you that everything will be alright if you take this risk – that your life will be full of friends and relations if you answer this call. But, do not believe me – you must take this step unassisted. The tears are just part of the movement into this space and they are the proof of your opening. They are impermanent, and they will be replaced by laughter. This journey, this work – is not optional. It is a required course – it is required of us all."

On the drive back to the office Adam pondered the beautiful Justine and the meaning of the phone number on the card. In the last thirty years he had noticed pretty women and, though tempted from time to time, he had never cheated on his marriage. He assumed the same was true of Cherie – besides how would she find time for another when she could not find time for him? But the mind that came to undermine his best intentions, continued to churn this latest development. He certainly was within his rights to seek a little comfort elsewhere; he had suffered long enough. No one would blame him. Cherie should be happy about it since he would stop bugging her for attention.

Back at the shop, Adam waded through the usual drama until the end of his shift. The elation he had felt with Justine was quickly fading. Phil was all over him about the crew goofing off, hurrying and finishing a task so they could hang out and smoke cigarettes and drink coffee.

Adam tried to clarify. "That's why they call them breaks."

Phil was fuming, "Couldn't we lock up the break room and open it just at designated times; and we have got to make sure they are held to fifteen minutes – if they go over by five seconds, that's company time and it's just stealing, pure and simple."

Adam explained that he was going to do nothing about Phil's concerns. That he actually believed everything was fine, and he did not want to fix something that was not broken.

Phil started to turn red. "I'll order them myself. I'm their boss. They work for me."

Adam was calm. "Problem is, Phil, I already told them not to take orders from you . . . chain of command, and all that."

"They have to listen to me. I can fire them. A can fire them all!"

"Boy, you would think so, but it would get real messy. I would just tell corporate they were following my orders. Then they would have cause to seek damages . . . open up the company to widespread litigation. Corporate would be very unhappy . . . wonder why you can't control your own employees."

"Fine, I'll just fire you."

Adam was cheerful. "At least make it about something important . . . like picking up trash."

"Don't think I won't. One day you're going to push me too far. And speaking of trash, we've got to do something about the garbage runs."

The resort hired more or less responsible high school kids for partial shifts to come in after school and pick up trash and collect all the garbage bags from the outdoor receptacles. There were usually two of them and they would sweep across the resort ending up at the large bins where they would drop all their findings.

Phil hated the idea of anyone enjoying his work. The kids, usually juniors or seniors, would ride a golf cart and chat it up while they swept the grounds. Adam knew the visiting slowed down the task a negligible amount, but actually loved the idea that such drudgery could be enjoyable for these lads. He tried to explain to Phil that having a little fun might make them do better work and keep them around longer. They were paid next to nothing, which they were happy to collect for buying themselves a soda and fast-food now and then.

This exchange of management theories elicited the usual belittling response from Phil. He thought every human being was basically slothful and would revert back to their natural state if they were not constantly monitored and shamed into giving back to the company the pound of flesh they had promised when they signed the employment contract.

Adam said, "I find that sometimes if a worker feels good about their job and likes their employer, they won't want to rip us off."

Phil countered, "Yeah, they like you. That's the problem."

Phil kept his numbers up at the resort by riding everybody hard and draining the last drop of energy out of each of them by the end of their shift. He looked good on paper and the parent company rewarded him with bonuses and increasingly better titles and salaries. They did not seem to notice that the turnover at the resort was staggering. They were constantly hiring, constantly training, constantly firing and losing employees, constantly short-staffed, and working harder to make up for the dwindling crews.

The culture that Phil created made Adam's job harder because Phil was always going behind his back and pissing off one his guys. Adam would have to step in and try to smooth things over and compensate for the erratic behavior of the mad dictator – and Phil would acknowledge that was Adam's job, although there was never a pat on the back.

On his way home, Adam stopped in again at the Corner Bar looking for Bud. He did not frequent the local watering hole, and he had a nagging fear that he might be developing a bad habit. Bud was warming his usual stool and Adam pulled in beside him and ordered a pint.

Bud was quick with a jab. "Hey, that's a pretty big beer. You know they have lady's sizes. Looks like you're becoming a regular. Welcome to the club."

"Yeah, that kind of worries me. Lately I need a little something before I head home."

Bud tried to be helpful. "Still having trouble with the wife? I'm here for you, man."

Adam volunteered that he had moved into the guest room. "She didn't even say a word, like she didn't notice. I've been on the couch before . . . but this is different. It feels permanent. We've got to make some big changes . . . or it's all over."

"You need another beer. It will help."

Adam was inconsolable. "It'll help . . . but it won't be enough."

The two discussed the southward trend in the longevity of marriage until Adam remembered why he had sought out his friend.

Adam pulled a sheet of paper out of his shirt pocket. "It's the plans for a Cajon."

Bud glanced at the page. "Cojones?"

"Just one – Cajon. It's a wooden box drum. I found it on the internet – downloaded the plans. It's cool and fun. I figure Leo can play it when we practice."

Bud was trying to be practical. "You sure that's such a good idea?"

"Yeah, if you watch your language."

Bud was dismayed, "Shit!"

"Do you think you can make one? I'll help."

Bud studied the plans. "It looks simple. Does it really make a drum sound?"

Adam was excited. "Let's try it out. I want to surprise him."

"Okay, I'm in.

Adam hesitated to relay his story. "And, speaking of the kid . . . I went to see the social worker.

Bud said, "So?"

"So . . . she's pretty."

Now he had Bud's attention. "You kidding me? What's she look like?"

"I don't know. There was something about her. I'm thinking, Susan Sarandon with dark hair and eyes. And something else; something I can't name."

Bud was subtle and mature, "Oh my God, you like her!"

Adam wanted to calm him down but couldn't help piling on. "Man, I don't even want to show you."

Adam pulled the business card out of his pants pocket and showed it to his friend. Bud studied it for a while. "Justine . . . that's pretty."

Then when he noticed it, "What's that? A phone number? Holy crap, jackpot!"

Adam contained himself. "It doesn't mean anything."

"It's a home phone number! You know how hard it is to get a home number? No, you don't know. You'll have to take my word."

"She just wants me to be able to reach her if something happens. Something could happen."

Bud was adamant. "Call her now. Call her right now! You can use my phone. Strike while the iron's hot."

"There is no iron and there will be no striking. I'm not going to call her. That would be an abuse of privilege."

Bud was beside himself. "Man, you're killing me."

"You're disgusting."

"It's my way." Bud was unapologetic as he took a long draw on his beer.

Adam shoved the card back into his pocket.

When Adam arrived home Cherie was still at the office. He shed himself of every thought of work, of Leo, of Bud, of Justine. He made his way to the kitchen to fix some dinner. Maybe he would surprise the little woman with something special. Perhaps some attention toward his wife would purge the impure thoughts he was having about the social worker lady. He chopped onions and garlic and dropped them into olive oil. The kitchen was soon perfumed with the pungent aroma.

He could not help but smile thinking of his Justine. My God! Did he really think that she was his? She was certainly not his, and the idea of owning her was abhorrent to him. He would not dream of holding down or restricting that spirit in any way, though his mind would come in here and fantasize about keeping her and protecting her. Did he think she would want to be protected?

His reverie was interrupted by the arrival home of Cherie. Adam knew that she was pulling away from him even more as he became more vocal about his dissatisfaction with their life. He could not imagine that she did not agree that there was something wrong, but he knew they would never agree on what was wrong or what the possible solutions might be. He did not begrudge her falling away from him though he still feared the loneliness that would surely follow. He could not deny that thoughts about Justine had buoyed him. He thought of her smile, those eyes, and that one simple touch to his arm. That meant nothing – no, it meant nothing – probably.

The red sauce was finished and he dropped the pasta, Cherie's favorite meal. This would be nice for her and take his mind off . . . Justine. Cherie made her hello's as she entered, shedding her briefcase and blazer, not filling the room with her usual chatter.

Adam tried to engage her. "Saw the social worker today. She says I'm here to save the kid – sad – guess there's nobody else – doesn't mean anything – just keep doing what I'm doing. She was amazing – really. Very smart. She made me think that I was doing something important."

He paused. "I haven't felt like that in a long time. Adam let a silence fall between them. Cherie looked at him like she was seeing him for the first time, then she broke the trance.

"You like her!"

Adam said, "What?"

"Oh my God, you like her! Think I can't live with you for thirty years and not know when you like somebody. For God's sake Adam, you're not in junior high."

He defended himself like he was in junior high. "I don't like her. She's just nice – you know, professional."

"Yeah, you like her because she's . . . professional. Oh my God, what does she look like?"

"Of course that's what you want to know. You don't want to know does she have a nice personality? Does she do a good job?"

"Right, you like her for her personality. Really, what does she look like?"

"She's not my type anyway. I'm sure she's older than me – but, you know – well preserved."

"Well preserved – that's just great."

"I'm surprised you care."

Cherie glared at him, her resentment building.

Adam was done with this. "I made pasta, my red sauce – it's your favorite."

She was cool to him, dismissive. "Yeah, well, I've got to watch my carbs. I'm doing a cleanse."

Adam counter punched, "Yeah, me too."

When Cherie retreated to her office, Adam pulled the business card out of his pocket and studied it.

FIVE – THE REBEL

The next card read "The Rebel." He instantly flashed on his former self – the one from college who seemed to stand against convention. She let him soak it in. The image was a grown man with long flowing hair that morphed into the wings of a Golden Eagle. His brightly colored cloaks were wrapped around him almost snake-like and he was stepping without effort through broken chains, a torch in his left hand and the sun upon his shoulder. He wanted to be this man, to reclaim this man. The reader spoke softly, "This is who you are – it is time for your return."

After school, Adam picked up Leo and drove out to the storage lot. The air was clean and the sky was pale blue. They were tearing out the old beds and building new platforms. There would be an adult double bed, all the space would allow. He was conscious that the bed was not big enough for he and Cherie – but for God's sake – it was just camping. Cherie had found the Airstream in the first place because she was tired of him dragging her into the woods, but Adam savored those memories.

When they were courting, just discovering each other, he introduced her to her first camping experience. They would load all the gear into his car and head into the Poudre National Forest. It was beautiful there – they had seen moose in the wild, they could hear the rush of an undammed river from the comfort of a blow-up mattress inside a cozy three-man dome tent. The three-man version was a concession to Cherie's delicate sensibilities. Before that, he had only used a rather small two-man backpacking tent; he felt the upgrade was spacious and luxurious.

When Adam had explained the upgrade to her, Cherie imagined the large safari tents she had seen in movies – the ones with flaps and kerosene lanterns, cots and side tables – the kind of tent that would be lugged into the clearing by dark skinned natives. When Adam finished erecting the small dome, she looked down on it and asked, "This is a three man tent? How do you stand up?"

He laughed. "It's for sleeping, babe. "

He took in the totality of the vast National Forest with a sweep of his arms. "This is our sitting room, this is our dining room, and that is the parlor."

Cherie eyed him with suspicion.

That evening, Adam set Cherie into a canvas camp chair while he grilled chicken breasts over the campfire. He brought her a real wine glass filled with a nice chardonnay.

He was cheery. "And I've got Caesar salad with my own dressing and hand grated parmigiana."

They sat with plates of savory food on their laps and their wine glasses resting on a small table between them. Cherie seemed to be won over.

She said, "You're right honey; this is fun."

The sun was setting quickly and the dusk overcame their clearing in the forest. Their dinner was lit up by a roaring campfire that Adam had re-stoked after cooking, and he raised his glass to her.

"Bon appetite!"

They both chuckled and settled into a warm and easy energy. They finished eating and were sipping the last of the bottle of wine when they noticed the sky canopy had become completely black except for flecks of stars.

Adam was first to notice the night sky. "My God, look at the stars."

Cherie noticed. "They're so bright. I didn't know they could be so bright."

Adam was a frequent camper and he could not recall such a sky. He said, "It must be a new moon. The only light is starlight."

He pointed to the sky and Cherie followed the line from his finger to the heavens. "That's the Milky Way. Do you see where it looks cloudy? It's just made up of tiny distant stars . . . thousands . . . must be millions. All together, they make the night sky milky."

Cherie was entirely with him. "I never knew why."

"All those tiny spots of light . . . it looks like dust."

Cherie completed the thought, excitedly. "Stardust!"

Adam stood and moved away from the glow of the campfire so he could get a better look. He pulled Cherie with him. He was overcome by the sight, reaching his hand over his head. "It feels like you could reach out and touch them."

Cherie said, "It makes you feel so small."

Adam pondered that thought for a moment. "That's what they say. I don't know . . . somehow . . . it makes me feel so big, like I'm a part of it."

Adam thought to himself, "I belong to planets and stars and supernovas. I was a fine hair on the hand that set it all in motion."

This last part he thought but did not speak, keeping a portion of the sensation to himself. He had an overwhelming feeling of connection to something huge, something enormous. Call it God, call it Universe – it doesn't matter. He felt a welling of emotion which he could not give to words. It was beyond words. He was born for this – something good, something great – he did not know what. But, he was sure it was coming to him – he just had to be prepared to see it and accept it when it arrived. He had to make room. He had to create space for the tremendous gifts the Universe was pouring out for him. He was in awe of the sight and standing in the darkness, pulled Cherie to his chest.

"Have you ever seen such a thing?"

Cherie was in this with him, he felt assured – she was his companion. They would travel this sky together – they would become great. He felt wetness gather in his eyes and he pulled her closer to him. He was sure she saw it too, she felt it too, she was right here with him, right where they belonged. But he did not share his tears, his tiny "man tears" with her.

Adam turned her to face him. "Look at you. I can see you. You are lit by starlight. Look how beautiful you are. Can you see me?"

She said, "I can see you too. I love you so much."

He held her close against him. "This is for us, baby. It's just for us. The sky is opening up for us . . . we just have to receive it. Can you feel it?"

Cherie snuggled into his embrace, her face against his heart. She said softly, "I can feel it. It's just for us."

That night in the forest, they listened to two coyotes calling to each other. They were on opposite ends of the campground. One would make its mournful cry and before long the other would answer. Adam felt there was magic in this but Cherie felt only fear. At one point she had to relieve herself, and made Adam go outside with her and stand by her on the edge of the clearing while she squatted – the coyotes still providing a soundtrack to the adventure. Adam was overcome with the humor of the situation and could not stop chuckling; Cherie, not so much. On the way home in the car, Cherie announced this would be her last time in a tent – ever. It was.

Adam held the business card in his hand a long time before he made the call and he had no idea what he would say. His wife's words reverberated in his head: "Oh my God, you like her." To him it seemed like it would be a good idea to touch base with her – talk about Leo – he was feeling kind of insecure – now that he thought about it – not sure he knew what in the hell he was doing – might be in over his head. Would it be okay if they had coffee – somewhere – there was a place not far from her office – her building made him anxious, somehow – would that be okay? It would.

Getting to the coffee shop early, Adam scouted out a good spot where he could see Justine enter. She appeared in the doorway like an apparition. Coming in out of the sunlight she glanced around while her eyes adjusted to the dimmer light. He watched, waiting for her to order. He fidgeted in his seat trying to get comfortable, trying to look casual, disinterested – and sucked in his gut a little. She noticed him at the corner table, and with a big smile, headed toward him. He had to get a hold on himself – she's just some woman, a government worker, nothing more. She sat down and he asked her what she was drinking. Green tea, of course. He had gotten a cappuccino and now wondered if it would give him bad breath.

He stood to shake her free hand. "Thanks so much for meeting me here. That government building kind of gives me the creeps."

She agreed. "Yeah, me too."

Adam started, "Well, after out talk . . . I guess I was kind of thrown. You know . . . kind of freaked out."

She replied, "Didn't mean to freak you out."

He defended, "You didn't. I mean it wasn't you. I freaked myself out. I'm not sure you got the right impression of me."

She tried to reassure him. "I'm sure you're doing just fine."

There was the smell of fresh ground coffee in the air and the sound of a barista frothing some milk. He decided to be honest. "I got into this match out of desperation. I was looking for some meaning in my life – I admit it. It was more for me, than for him."

Justine paused and thought before speaking. "At least you're honest about it."

"It's just that it's turned into something else . . . something more. I feel like I should be more transparent."

She was surprised. "Really?"

Adam had a confession. "I didn't lie to you, but . . . my wife and I . . . well, we're probably not the best role models for Leo. I mean, as a couple . . . we're not at our best."

Justine tried to reassure him, "I already had a sense of that, from before. It's not what you said. It's what you didn't say."

"I knew that you knew. I just wanted you to know that I knew that you knew."

Justine sat back a little and sipped her tea. "Well, that wasn't needed. But, thanks."

They sat and started to learn about each other. He wanted her to talk about herself, but she didn't let that go too deep. Instead she gave him room, gave him license to talk about his life. He hated his job – yes, he knew that was a cliché. He thought he would be doing something important by this time in his life; he wondered if it was too late. He remembered that night in the forest when he felt connected to everything. He told her about it, but he didn't tell her everything.

She sensed there was still much unsaid. She stared into her teacup for a time, then raised her head and fixed him with her eyes. Seemingly, out of the blue she asked, "So, what is your spiritual practice?"

He was stunned, "What?"

Nonchalantly, she clarified, "You said you were looking for meaning. I think that's what you're talking about. What do you do to nurture that connection? What is your practice? Go to church? Meditate? Yoga? What do you do?"

He was stunned. "It is what I'm talking about. I'm just not used to talking about it . . . to anyone. It's California, you know. We're politically correct."

"Oh, yeah – I forgot. I don't pay much attention to that. Everybody's got a spiritual practice, whether they know it or not. I think there's value in laying it out – giving it some air."

Adam loved her boldness, her aura of abandon and fearlessness. He laughed. "We tried church; it didn't take. Cherie still goes sometimes – to network."

"I didn't ask what *we* do – I asked what *you* do."

He laughed again, nervous. "I used to be the seeker. I took classes on religion and philosophy. I still read the books: Deepak, Wayne Dyer. It all resonates with me.

Adam paused a moment. "I guess I got lost."

Justine refocused him. "Or fell asleep."

It fit for him. "Yes, that's it. That's exactly it."

She was encouraging. "Good news. It's not too late."

"Jeez, I hope not." He continued, "I was attracted to some eastern practices but really never took the plunge. I even heard there's a Buddhist retreat in Marin – read about it in the paper – sounded cool."

She knew the place. "I go there sometimes, very calming. You have to do something – don't call it effort. You have to let the effort fall away then what remains is peace."

He looked at her in awe. "I can't believe you know about this stuff."

"I know all kinds of stuff – you would be surprised."

"I'm not surprised."

Justine said, "I know what it feels like to be dissatisfied with your situation. You know, you can have your peace, your true purpose anywhere, anyplace. But, sometimes the place can't hold you, or can't keep you – literally can't provide you with your sustenance."

"Like a job your hate."

"Yes, but for me it's not the job. Still, I'm leaving the state, already given notice."

He didn't like this development. "You're done with California?"

"More like, California's done with me. It's just time to go."

He questioned, "Where?"

"Not far . . . Arizona . . . Sedona. There's something for me there . . . don't know what it is exactly . . . I'll find out."

"You have a job there?"

"No . . . something will come to me."

"How can you do that?"

She found his eyes. "How can you not?"

She gave him the phone number for the meditation retreat in Marin. He had meditated before but never stuck with it.

Still he was a believer – he told himself it had nothing to do with her, but he made a mental note of the date she was headed to the center. He had surreptitiously found it on the page of her date book when she rummaged in her purse for the phone number. It was stamped in his brain, in bold letters. It felt sneaky.

She had to give him one last warning. "You need to know . . . if you go . . . this is not all fun and games. It's not a spa, no frills, no massage, no room service. There's a little instruction and a lot of quiet time. Sure you're up for that?"

He was sure. "Are you kidding? That sounds like heaven. It's exactly what I want. I'm there – I'm starting today."

From his office he made the reservation: simple quarters; scheduled group meditation time; individual meditation time; communing with nature; no drugs, no alcohol; and, very little interaction with others – don't know about that, she would be there.

Meditation became Adam's new obsession. At home that night, he sat on a pillow in the bedroom, put on a George Winston CD, closed his eyes, and cleared his mind. No thought. No thought. He breathed in deeply, held it, and exhaled – and all he could see was her.

SIX – THE MASTER

The next card was the master himself. Adam had seen his face before (would have been the metaphysical bookstore in Boulder) but he never took any interest. The Guru peered at him from the darkness surrounded by a grove of trees with bare branches. A full moon overhead illuminated the face. He waited for the reader to speak. "You are in need of teachers – there will be many. But, the true master lives in you.

Everything you need to know is available to you at the core of your being. Everything you seek, already exists – you just need to let your misperceptions fall away. When you let go of illusion, you will be left with the eternal – it's the only thing that's real. It's like Dorothy and the ruby slippers: you had them all along."

Life before Cherie – he tried to remember. Why was his mind taking him here? Or was it his heart? Good, he thought, that he could not tell. He had been a whole person, full of confidence, self assured. She had not driven that out of him – he knew that. Whatever had caused the change had come from him alone. Now he felt guilty to have blamed her – that's what they did, they blamed each other. It was a deadly spiral downward, a game neither one could win.

But, that boy – before Cherie – longed for solitude and did not fear it. He did not stay with someone because he was afraid to be alone. There were other girls, nice girls, and he loved them all – loved them still. And it was always he who ended it, always he who did the dirty work, pointing out with all the kindness he could muster, that they did not belong together. No, he did not know why – but he knew it with certainty. And they would cry, or call, or leave ginormous letters on his door. He longed to be alone for awhile, and he savored the time, sometimes going on camping trips, or solo road trips he would call a vision quest. Those times would invigorate him, bring him to himself.

He loved the company of women – always better with women than with men. His friendship with Bud was an aberration, perhaps forced because he felt it was strange he had so few male friends. It was unnatural. Guys were supposed to get together and watch football, and drink beer, talk about hot babes, tell off-color jokes. He could do all that, but never sought out that kind of company.

Even in college when his male roommates explored the limits of debauchery, he became the contrary, the one who kept his head while all others were happily losing theirs. He was the one who could quote Thoreau, and discuss politics, playwrights, and art. He even cooked, and that had gotten the attention of the girls.

He loved to cook for women, maybe one special woman at a time. They were amazed by this turn, and this behavior had garnered positive results. Women liked him. He wasn't a jock but he could hold his own on a tennis court or in a pick-up game of basketball. What he lacked in natural ability he made up for in intensity and hustle. So, some women, not all, liked it that he could show some softness.

He was monogamous once a union was begun; this also felt right and natural to him. There might have been a time or two when there was a slight overlap, but his guilt over these indiscretions gave him proof that his intentions were pure. There might have been a time or two when he had to break off a relationship quickly so he could start up a new one without guilt.

The constant during this time before Cherie, was that he preferred to be alone. So when he wanted companionship, all he ever had to do was step outside his solitude, and there was always someone there. He never doubted that if he wanted a woman, he would have one. That assurance was long gone. Now he was thinking it would be good to find a backup before he did anything drastic.

He could not imagine Cherie would be upset at ending this thing. She seemed to be already heading for the exit. Of course she would be pissed if she didn't think it was her idea. She would be upset about the additional duty a separation or divorce might bring. He still wasn't sure he could do it anyway – and there was no small part of fear in facing her with this. She might kill him – or try.

Today, Cherie left work early in order to spend exactly a half-day in the garden. She wanted it to look just so when they had visitors and clients over. But, it also gave her deep ease to pull weeds, to plant things, to put her gloved hands in the soil. It was really her only spiritual practice; and, though she complained about Adam's lack of assistance here, she relished spending the time alone.

Today she had a large flat of blue and pink petunias. They would accent at least half a dozen beds around the yard, a quick splash of color that would bloom the entire summer. Badger followed her around, asking for attention, receiving a cursory pat on the head and a, "Now, go lie down – I've got work to do."

Badger found a cool patch of grass, made three turns, and settled himself into a circle of dog.

Cherie pushed her trowel into the prepared soil of the bed that bordered the flagstone patio. It was during these times that she would contemplate her life, their life. She knew her husband was restless and feared what he might do. Didn't he see that she was also deeply unhappy? But her mind would not let her find the cause. Was it Adam and his seemingly endless stream of "mid-life" crises? Was it the demanding schedule she kept at the realty office, scrambling to keep ahead of the other agents? Was it her own lack of purpose, or the additional three pounds that had mysteriously appeared on her carefully monitored waist?

She needed a massage – and a day at the spa (maybe a half-day). She needed a cut and a color, a mani-pedi for sure, maybe a facial. When was the last time she took some time for herself?

She adjusted the wide brimmed hat that kept the sun from marring her fine features and took in the whole panorama of the back yard. It looked good – maybe good enough – but far from finished. All she could see was what was left undone. All she could see were the hours of labor that lie before her, before she might find rest. She could not enjoy what had already been accomplished. She stopped and felt into this thought and knew it wasn't quite right. But, the arrival of Adam's pickup in the driveway kept her from going any further, any deeper.

He was surprised to find his wife in the garden, taking time off from work, but he didn't say so. Badger greeted him like he'd been gone for years and Adam gave the dog a much needed rubbing, from ears to belly. Then, he helped Cherie find a home for the last of the petunias and listened to her list of plans for the yard – couldn't he prune the hedges tomorrow? They cleaned the tools and set them in the garden shed that matched the architecture of the house. This was nice – just working together. It was not intimacy – they were not exactly connecting. But, it was nice.

When he told Cherie about the meditation retreat, she shook her head. "How'd you get off work?"

"Took a vacation day. Boy, Phil is not happy. I don't give a crap. He won't fire me. He can't. But, he made me take one day as leave without pay. Asshole."

"So this is costing us more than just the price of the spa weekend."

"It's a retreat. Very Spartan, no frills, no massage – they're monks for God's sake. Besides, you're going to talk to me about spending money?"

He was trying to be ironic.

She changed the subject. "So, is <u>she</u> going to be there?"

Adam pretended he didn't know to whom she was referring. "She who?"

"She. Your little girlfriend, the social worker."

"No, of course not." he lied. Justine didn't even know he was going. What in the hell was he doing?

When Adam checked into the Buddhist center, "Spartan" certainly seemed to be the operative word. His room was clean but bare, with a cot, a small table, and a chair – everything he could possibly need. The restroom facilities were in another building and were communal, one side for men, the other for women. He remembered that he had complained about not being able to go camping anymore. He unpacked and sat for a moment, collecting his thoughts. He reasoned that the real purpose for his stay was to center himself, to really learn some methods – his intentions were pure. Justine might not even show up, they had not coordinated anything – he was doing nothing wrong.

The retreat center quartered a handful of real monks who lived there, maintained the facility and the grounds, and led the meditation sessions. They were an austere group whose smiles were slight, who moved from task to task with apparent ease. Adam envied them and their simple life. The grounds were natural and beautiful. They were close enough to the ocean that they received almost daily fog and mist. There were huge Coastal Oaks and Eucalyptus, with ferns underneath, and a myriad of plants and flowers he could not name. The place celebrated the color green and, taking in the hillside, Adam convinced himself he was here for an innocent purpose.

A bell sounded and he proceeded to the meditation room. Tomorrow they would do this outside, but to get started they wanted no distractions. Inside, the room had bare bamboo floors. The ones ahead of him, seeming to know the drill, each picked up a folded blanket, then setting it on the floor, sat cross-legged facing the instructor. He was a monk, only slightly Asian, shaved head, with an expressionless face. Adam took his blanket and found a spot with a clear view of the door coming in. He pretended to stretch his neck a little, to settle himself. He pretended to close his eyes like the others, to center himself, to prepare.

As the instructor began the session – she still had not entered. Didn't matter – he was here for himself.

The monk directed them to close their eyes and focus on their breath. "Breathe in deeply through the nose, a cleansing breath, and hold it. Release it through your mouth. Again, breathe deep, and this time focus your attention on the out-breath. This is the breath that takes you closer to the Divine. Your last breath will be an out-breath."

The thought was slightly unsettling for Adam, but he concentrated on the breath, and a shudder ran up his spine and across his shoulders. It was a vibrant, alive feeling and he wondered what it was and from where it came. They were given a few more words and an image – a flower opening to the sun – yes, that feels right. Then, they were left on their own to shed their thoughts, to let the images and thoughts slide easily into their consciousness, then to let them slip away. He did not peek, and he did his best to maintain the image of the flower. He tried not to try.

At the end of the session, he felt transformed – he had almost forgotten about looking for her. The attendees filed out of the room heading for their simple lodging. There was almost no visiting – an unspoken code of silence – nothing to disturb the initiates on their journey inward. In silence, he made his way back to his room. He was overcome by a feeling of peacefulness.

That's when he saw her. She was standing before a flowering tree in just enough light from a distant bulb that it was unmistakably her. He stopped. She had already seen him but did not move from her place. Who would move first? He concluded quickly, it would have to be him, but he wished it was her.

He walked to her slowly, gently; she didn't say a word.

He could not interpret her mood. "A very good session just now," he said. "Transformative, really. You should have been there."

There was still no response – not anger that he had followed her here. He could not lie, now; it was stupid to try. She could look straight into him and know everything; he was an open book.

She spoke. "Why are you here?"

"It was your recommendation . . . I really do need this. Just now . . . I really got into it."

"But that's not why you're here."

He admitted, "No."

She kept up her gaze – looking at him, through him. And all he could do was bare himself to her scrutiny. He had no defense, no excuse.

He said, "I'm sorry."

"If you wanted to talk to me, I would do that. What did you think would happen here? We're surrounded by monks for God's sake."

"I can't say what I was thinking. I thought maybe in a neutral setting, maybe in a beautiful place like this . . . I don't even know. I wanted you to see who I really am . . . what I really am. I thought maybe. . . ."

"What you really are . . . is married."

He tried to explain. "My marriage is over."

"I've got a feeling your wife is unaware of this."

"She knows it's over, she just won't say so."

Justine was finished. "This is over too, all of this. I'm going home. You stay and have your retreat – you need it more than I do."

As she moved to leave he held out his hand. She stopped, but did not take it. She was looking away from him, to some distant mark. He took her hand gently, just holding it – she let him. He raised the joined hands slowly and held them to his chest – his intention was pure. She turned to him and he was surprised to see tears. He could not have caused this; he hated that he might have brought her sadness. He wanted to say he was sorry. He wanted to go to his knees and beg forgiveness. He touched his free hand to her face and wiped away a tear –

she almost smiled. He bent his face to hers and kissed her lips, just once.

Now, she pulled away slowly and made her way to that mark she had set for herself. She glided through a shaft of moonlight as she went and he could make out the dampness on her cheek. He raised his hand to his face, and felt the same.

SEVEN – TRUST

This card was called "Trust." It showed a vaguely female form in free-fall with bare outstretched arms, black hair trailing behind her. Adam questioned: "Is she falling or is she flying?" The card gave him a feeling of peacefulness.

The reader spoke, "Notice she is gliding from the deep blue of the sky which represents Source into the rosy rays of morning – it is the promise of a new beginning. This is where you will land but you must do what the card commands – Trust."

Adam felt a sadness that actually helped him purge his guilt around Justine. And he could not forget the fleeting touch, the kiss. He had stayed through the end of the retreat and he felt like a new being. He brought his practice home and set up a space for himself in his bedroom, the reclaimed guest room. He tried to explain nothing, and Cherie was resigned to shaking her head and mumbling.

Shortly after his return from the retreat, Adam went into his wife's bedroom to retrieve some more clothes and some toiletries. When Cherie came in, he felt caught, out of place. With his hands in a dresser drawer, he explained, "I was just getting some clothes."

Cherie quickly busied herself with some straightening. "Sure, I was just . . . well, I live here."

Adam felt unaccountably embarrassed. "Sure . . . of course."

The lilting sound of contemplative music was drifting into the room from Adam's boom-box, punctuated by the nearly inaudible chanting of "Om-m-m." Cherie noticed. "Is that . . . did you bring your meditation home?"

Adam laughed nervously. "Trying to. Trying not to think, you know."

Cherie raised an eyebrow. "I guess only one of us needs to think."

Adam tried to clarify. "I'm trying not to try."

"Good luck with that."

"It's good stuff. You should give it a try."

"I do sometimes. We always have a meditation at the close of our Pilates workout. He's really a yoga instructor, so he's all about the meditation. It's good. Sometimes I have to leave early."

Adam paused. "So . . . you're doing alright?"

Cherie answered without conviction. "I'm great."

Adam pulled the last of his socks from the drawer and closed it. "Good . . . I'm just getting some stuff. I better get to it . . . before the CD stops."

They smiled politely to each other as Adam left the room. They were moving away from each other like freight trains racing toward opposite coasts.

He didn't try to contact Justine, and she didn't call. He did not try to move out of the sadness; to him that would have spelled finality. He wanted to hold onto this last memory of her – he carried it with him, he kept it in his awareness.

74

Unconsciously, his hand would wander to his chest and it all would come rushing back causing him to catch his breath and choke back tears. Sometimes in the car, when no one could see, he would let the tears fall down. It felt good to be sad, over her. This was his rebirth, maybe his awakening. He was unattaching himself from Justine, but he was coming to a deeper sense of self.

He attacked the Airstream with new enthusiasm, Leo at his side. The platform beds were built. The dining table broke down to form a twin bed for a single sleeper. Leo knew the bed was his and he took special care in sanding the oak trim and applying the urethane. They refinished all the cabinets and pulled up the cracked and faded tiles. They glued down a nice piece of good outdoor carpet, a remnant from someone's spa remodel.

They laid down good vinyl in the bathroom, hung a shower rod, and made sure all the moving parts would move. The new water pump insured that they could camp without a hookup and still have water. A new marine battery powered the lights, the pump, and the hydraulic winch that raised and lowered the tongue. They were close to making a test run.

Leo was hand polishing a shine back onto the aluminum skin of the once silver beast. Adam stopped to admire their progress. He said, "It's looking good."

Leo was anxious. "We've been at this for months. When's the camping trip."

Adam thought out loud, "I don't know. We need four new tires; I guess I can do that before the weekend."

Leo perked up. "The weekend?"

"We're not quite done, but we might be close enough for a trial run."

Leo did not want to miss this opening. "I can come over every day after school. If you wrote me a note, I could skip school."

Adam laughed, "You're not skipping school. We'll make it alright. And we have practice with the band tonight – did you forget? Me and Bud built a drum for you – it's really cool."

"You want me to be the drummer?"

"I thought you knew that."

"I thought you were kidding."

"No way, kid. This is your big shot. You're in."

Leo hesitated. "I don't even know if I can play."

"It's easy. You'll just keep a rhythm . . . you know . . . with your hands. It'll be a snap for you."

Leo saw another opening. "It's because I'm black, isn't it?"

Adam laughed hard. "Yes, because you're black. Do you think you can keep a beat?"

Adam snapped his fingers, creating a rhythm. "Just like that!"

Leo took up the cadence, slapping the side of the pickup with his hands. He sang, "I can do that."

That evening Adam brought Leo to Bud's garage for his first go-round with the abbreviated band. Bud presented the

Cajon like he was unveiling a sculpture. It was shiny brown, a perfect rectangular box, just high enough for Leo to sit on comfortably.

Bud was proud of the workmanship. "I just put on the final coat last night. You couldn't buy a better one."

Leo took the box drum and sat it on the floor. "Whoa, this is cool." He was anxious to get started as he immediately progressed to experimenting with the sounds. He tapped on the thin front with his palms; with his fingers he drummed the sides and the corners. "C'mon you guys; get suited up!"

Adam and Bud strapped on their guitars and adjusted the amps. Without tuning, Adam started an upbeat melody; Bud joined him on the bass. Leo struggled to find the groove, but then settled in. He let the music wash over him, he shut his eyes and he slipped into the flow. Without trying too hard, he found his part. The three musicians spoke to each other with their independent sounds, finding an easy conversation.

Bud yelled at Leo, "Go, Leo! Smack that son of a. . . ."

Adam interjected loudly, "Bud!"

Bud apologized. "Sorry, just got caught up."

Adam changed the rhythm slightly, adjusted the note progression with Bud and Leo following along. Suddenly Bud recognized the song and he volunteered the lyrics. He sang, "Up on Cripple Creek, you send me. If I spring a leak, you mend me. I don't have to speak, you defend me. A drunkard's dream if I ever did see one."

Somehow, it sounded just right. They laughed and they played, and in the night they entered a new dimension that held only three boys, testing the bonds of friendship; finding the edge of new ways to speak, new ways to love.

After the jam session Adam and Leo were still flying, chattering like little girls when they rolled into the house. They stopped short when they found Cherie at the kitchen table with a stack of papers. Leo squatted down to say hi to Badger and rub his back.

Adam brought her up to date. "Sorry Hun. I'm just dropping off some stuff before I take Leo home. You should have heard us tonight; we were rocking it out. And this guy can burn it up on the drum. Isn't that right, Leo?"

Leo was suddenly subdued. "Yeah, I guess so."

Cherie said, "So you had a good time."

Adam tried to pull her into the experience. "The best; we could play down at the tavern if we could figure out how to get Leo in."

"Good plan. Let's corrupt the kid . . . um . . . Leo."

Adam told Cherie about their progress on the Airstream and their intention to take it out for a test run. She tried to pay attention.

"I think next weekend me and Leo will take her over to the coast . . . shake out the cobwebs." He laughed. "Literally – there really are cobwebs."

"I can't believe Phil is giving you the time off."

"He's not. I'm just taking it. Don't worry, he'll make me pay for the time off, big time. You said I had to manage the manager – so I did."

"You are going to get yourself fired."

Adam laughed. "That's my plan."

Leo looked up, trying to understand the joke, but remaining low, under the line of fire. Cherie said, "That's not funny."

"No, it is funny. That would be the best news of the year, maybe the best news of the decade. I am not staying there, Cherie; I don't even care anymore. I'm on my way out – you need to get use to it."

Here it comes, the fear. "Then what the hell are you going to do? We've got bills to pay. You know we can't stay afloat without your salary, small as it is."

Leo stood up from petting the dog and the two seemed to suddenly notice he was in the room. He let them off the hook, saying, "I'll wait for you in the truck."

As the kid exited through the garage Adam assured him, "Hey I'll just be a minute. They waited until he was out of ear-shot then started in again. Adam, defensive, said, "Yeah, I get it – I've got a lousy job. Maybe I could get a better one."

"In this economy? You need to keep what you have – the time will come when you can branch out, look for something else."

"I'm not sure you are hearing me. This is not up for debate. No, Phil is not going to fire me; he won't. I've tried everything I know to make that happen – he just won't let me go. I have to quit."

Cherie said quietly, "This is a deal breaker, Adam."

Adam looked at her in silence, and then said, "If that's true, Cherie, we haven't got much to stand on."

"What does that mean?"

"It means, if making money and paying bills is the foundation of this marriage, then we don't have shit. That's not enough, that's not enough for me. Here's the deal breaker: I want more from my marriage. I do not want to just mark time – that's what they do in prison."

"I don't have time for this. This discussion is over."

Adam needed one more jab, "It's more than this discussion that's over."

They glared at each other, and then moved again to separate corners. They had reached an impasse. In Adam's mind the ball was in her court. She would have to do something – counseling, meditation – anything that would begin to wake her up. It would have to be something extraordinary.

Adam was glad to be spending a little more time with Leo as they headed for the foster home. It helped to dispel the toxic energy he felt, and Leo let him process in peace. He did not feel anger toward his wife, but a nagging sadness was clawing at him from the inside. It was a familiar feeling. He noticed that he had grown accustomed to its frequency, and marveled at his ability to stay with it.

It was a sunny day when the boys hitched up the Airstream to the Chevy pickup. Adam plugged the power line into the truck and tested the brake lights and the turn signals. There were amber running lights around the top of the trailer that came on only when the headlights were engaged. Adam thought all the lights should be on as they paraded through town heading south, looking for the highway to the coast.

Leo was noticeably animated. He had lived forty miles from the coast for much of his life and had never seen the Pacific Ocean. The road curved through redwood groves along the Russian River. They rolled down windows and let the scented air blow around the cab. Adam played Bruce Springsteen on the CD player and hummed along while Leo kind of be-bopped to the rhythm – not his kind of music – but, you know – got to humor the "old" man. Every ten minutes Leo would look back at the silver beast following patiently behind, and say, "I think it's gaining on us."

He would laugh at his own joke, then repeat it ten minutes later – and laugh again. Adam thought, "This is what it's all about – this is life living itself. Does it get any better?"

There were no hookups at the state beach so this would be what the old Airstream manual called "dry camping." They would have running water and limited use of the toilet. Too much use and they would have to drive somewhere and dump the 1970's smallish storage tank. They registered at the entrance to the park and found a spot where they could back in along a row of newer trailers. Their back window faced the Pacific Ocean and Adam could see the kid was impatient to run down and touch the water. Adam thought it was endearing that he stayed and did his work in setting up camp, catching glances over his shoulder at the waves crashing on the beach like they might just go away.

Finally, Adam couldn't stand it anymore, yelling, "Just go!" Leo bolted to the edge of the water, hesitated, then kicked off his shoes and waded in. Adam caught up with him after a few minutes, and did the same. They were two little boys seeing the ocean for the first time. They ran, they skipped, they splashed each other, laughing all the time. The intentioned wading became a total immersion and they were soaked when they wandered back to the trailer, exhausted.

Adam noticed he and Leo were collecting some stares from the other campers – they must look a sight. Adam rarely noticed the difference in their skin color and it made him uncomfortable to think that others did notice. Leo's question about perversion flashed briefly through his mind, making Adam laugh out loud. He waited for the kid to change into dry clothes before he took his turn inside the trailer.

They would take one more walk on the beach at dusk looking for the odd mussel shell but mostly looking for sea glass.

Adam explained, "It's probably a piece of a beer bottle." He held out the amber jewel in his hand. "See, the waves and the sand work against it until all the sharp edges are gone."

Leo took the piece of glass, studying it. "Cool." He scanned the water's edge, looking for another piece. When he saw one, he bolted. "There's one! I found one, look at it!"

Adam added to the challenge, "The hardest ones to find are blue. Try to find a blue one. They are mostly green and brown."

Leo became immersed in the game, finding the tiny shards and stuffing them into his pockets. "I'll bet I can find a bunch. What can we do with them?"

Adam bent to inspect something shiny. "We could make something . . . a collage . . . some kind of art piece. Or we could put them in a clear glass bowl . . . just to show.

Leo liked the idea. "There's another one! Where are the blue ones?"

The sun was setting fast and they stopped to watch the orange ball sink into the ocean. Adam said, "It's going to be dark before we eat. We'll have to make a fire. They trudged back to the campground in the last light of the day and Adam thought, "This feels like family."

Adam's "blood" family was far away tonight, in a small town in southern Illinois. He believed they had once been close, but time and circumstances had conspired to create distance between he and his sisters with their assorted nieces and nephews. Adam loved his sisters and credited them mainly with raising him up, in the absence of a father and in the presence of an indifferent mother.

His father had died quite young when Adam was just nine years old, and he still had ambiguous feelings about this mystical figure. Someone once said the best thing a father can do for his son is to die young. Adam did not have one negative memory of his father, and he wondered if this proverb where true. He never felt judgment from his father when he took a different road regarding politics and belief. He had none the gifts a father can give his son, but he also had none of the recriminations.

Adam saw many of his male friends seethe with resentment over the disapproval their fathers handed them, and he thought, "At least they have fathers." Now in the dawning of his middle age, Adam was aware that he carried around issues around abandonment. There was no doubt this insecurity stemmed from being left behind by a departing father, however righteous his excuse. So, Adam was left alone in a house full of women, and there was no man to take his side, when sides were taken.

Adam's mother had a strained relationship with her husband before he died. He had been dominant, probably domineering, and she resented being over-directed. When he passed on she felt a great weight lifted, but in her son's face she saw the father's likeness. Adam rationalized that his mother's neglect was entirely unconscious and he also had no other life-story available with which to make comparisons. He suspected it was natural for mothers to have preferred relationships with their daughters.

In his later life, Adam had surmised that his absent father and neglectful mother had unknowingly created an independent and self-sufficient adult. These were qualities he was proud of, and he rarely let himself take a deeper look at the feelings of hurt and inadequacy that percolated just beneath this façade of self confidence.

There were shadows here that would go undiscovered for decades, but they would raise their alarming heads now and then in Adam's quest for approval. They would find life in the intimate relationships he repeatedly fell into in an attempt to compensate for his lack of self-love. And these tendencies seemed to manifest themselves most dramatically in his relationships with women. He was still trying to get his sisters to play "army" with him, when they naturally preferred to play with Barbie's.

He became an effective manager. He was skilled in getting his teams to work together and have fun. He was building substitute families for himself – better ones – and he was good at it. He was using his own shadow to create light. He had genuine concern for the ones who worked for him, and they usually performed in their jobs just to win the approval of the best boss in the world. He was sometimes taken advantage of because he trusted too much and bent too far. And at the core of the effective manager was the shadow: the little boy who felt left out and needed others to like him; to validate him; to keep him company and to tell him he was okay.

Adam was the third child, and when the two older girls got jobs and got married, he had a season with his mother before he left home to go to college. He didn't figure it out until later, but with the other girls gone, his mother suddenly needed him. They had quality conversations about politics, religion, and life, while Adam was just starting to shape opinions on these topics.

He enjoyed forming this new relationship with his mother, forgetting that this was the same parent who the previous year had forgotten his birthday. On that day, when night fell and no one had remembered, he left a note on the refrigerator and went to bed. The following day, after school, there was a cake, and presents, and an abundance of guilty faces.

When he went off to college, the first in his family to do so, Adam made an effort to stay connected with his mother, sending her the occasional letter chronicling the life of a small town boy in the arena of higher learning. But, she didn't seem interested in his life now that it was outside her frame of reference. He wanted her to grow with him, to become more learned and aware of the wide world.

When Adam read that slim volume about unconditional love by Eric Fromm in one of his classes, he learned that real love encompassed acceptance and approval. He wrote his mother and apologized for failing to love her without conditions and promised to do better in the future. He felt his mother did not entirely understand what the "art" of love included even though she used the word freely and easily. He came right out and told her that he did not feel he had her acceptance and approval and he would like to have that now.

Most parents would have expressed their love even if they didn't believe it in the hearts. But his mother wrote back to tell him that only God could give him the approval he sought, and that he should not expect that from her. He thought, "Jesus, she could have just said the damn words. She could have lied. She didn't have to believe it."

Adam came to realize that his mother could not give him something she did not have. It made him sad to understand that she was so love-starved that she could not truly love any other person, even her children. He pitied her and forgave her. But, he did not want to ever go back to that well for something that would not be forthcoming, so he distanced himself from his family. He went home less and less. He didn't write, he didn't call; and no one seemed to notice.

This realization gave Adam the conviction that he needed to be the source for his own care and nurturing. He was convinced that he would be his own mother and his own father, and should never seek true acceptance outside of himself. He believed this with his mind, but to the mind it was only words. He continued to look for love in all the wrong places.

After school, Adam left the Midwest and never returned again except to visit. His sisters started their own families and seemed to gravitate emotionally further and further away from him and from each other. His mother became unwell and was not even able to travel to he and Cherie's wedding. After a prolonged illness his mother died. Adam felt empty inside when he heard the news, not sad, not angry. He stood and watched them lower her casket into the ground and thought: "just a wasted life." He thought she had lived her whole earthly existence and never experienced the authentic giving and receiving of love.

Now he had occasional contact with his sisters. The girls all lived within twenty miles of the small town in which they had grown up, and Adam was on the left coast, no doubt eating sprouts and smoking herb. He did not doubt their love for him, but he was outcast and absent, easily forgotten. When he was small he had hungered for their attention. Now, he tried to be satisfied with himself, alone. But there was a wounding around his relationship with them that was not quite alive in his awareness.

For Adam, the unusual family unit he was forging with Leo felt very satisfying. He didn't express this, because their future together was so uncertain, but he could not imagine the dissolution of this match. A part of him longed for family, and he resolved to call his sisters and to catch up with the nieces and nephews.

Back at the campsite, Adam set out a mason jar to hold the growing collection of sea glass. This would be a continuing project for the weekend and they would watch the pile of gems accrue. For dinner they roasted hotdogs on the ends of skewers and munched on potato chips; nothing gourmet for this party of two. Adam could have put together a rather gourmet spread but this felt just right: meat in the shape of a tube and s'mores for dessert. Adam played a little music on a portable player in the background, and they sat mostly quiet in their camp chairs, leaning back, looking at the night sky. Now and then Leo would rise to stir the coals – his job – or to throw on another log or pile of sticks. Adam thought it was probably his first campfire too, but didn't ask. He took to the tending like a pro and Adam pretended he was.

It felt late when they prepared for bed. The stars were glowing like the embers of their dying fire, much like that night in Colorado when Adam had felt so close to Cherie – and to God. He pointed out all the constellations that he knew with Leo commenting: "That don't look like no hunter – and that sure as hell don't look like no dog."

The dippers did look like dippers to Leo, but Adam rushed to say that they were really bears and the dipper name was an insult to a noble animal.

Adam said, "Look at them. See the long tail? Then the head is going to be at the other end."

Leo squinted and said, "Okay, I guess I can see it . . . now." He was also curious about Virgo the Virgin, asking, "How could you tell?"

Adam pointed out the Seven Sisters, pointing. "That cluster right there . . . see it looks like a small triangle. Now, count them. They're all sisters – the Pleiades. "

He studied the points of light. "I count five; no, six."

Adam helped him. "There should be seven. Some of them are very faint. They're called the Pleiades."

Leo sounded the word out slowly. He said, "Plee-a-dees. I see them now, seven."

He repeated, "Plee-a-dees." The word felt good in his mouth and he released it again, freeing it into the night sky where he imagined it floated up to the sisters and made them smile to be so noticed.

Adam got him to open up some more about his mother, Celeste. It was ironic that they were looking at celestial bodies and this kid's mother was anything but celestial. She was still in the county lock-up. Leo went to see her once a week – said she seemed good, sober at least. He said she would go on and on about what they would do when she got out – maybe move to Chicago – they had family there she said. Everything would be different – he'd see the change.

Leo was resigned to the fact that he would be in the foster home for the foreseeable future, and he was somewhat fatalistic about his mom's chances.

At the end of a long pause, Leo found the nerve to say, "Don't know why I can't live at your house . . . we're together all the time anyway . . . make it easier."

Adam had to collect his thoughts.

"That would be a big move, kid. I'm just a volunteer, already spending more time than I'm supposed to."

"I'd help out around the house – you know I'm a good worker."

Adam had to control his emotions. "You're the best ever. I'm already afraid I'm abusing the child-labor laws. I should be paying you. But you know how it is. . . ."

"No, I don't know how it is."

Adam rationalized, "The courts would be involved . . . have to jump through a million hoops. Not sure they'd even approve us."

Leo said it then: "Us. That's the reason – us. She doesn't like me."

"Cherie? Of course she likes you . . . don't be silly . . . she doesn't even know you."

"She could – if she wanted."

"Here's the God's honest truth, kid: we're not doing so good, me and the wife. That's why they wouldn't let us. You need to be in a stable home. I'm not sure me and Cherie are going to make it."

This at least, was the truth, and Leo shruggingly accepted it. But, it wasn't all the truth. Adam would have taken Leo in a flash if Cherie would cooperate. It nagged at him and haunted him that he would drop Leo off at the foster home he hated, after a day of joy. In his mind he set a goal, he would remedy this situation; it was only a matter of time.

That night, Leo bedded down on the twin, with Adam on the adult double bed. Adam was lying in Posturepedic luxury while Leo slept on the thinner foldaway mattress that stretched across the dining booth. Leo could not have been more comfortable at the Ritz. Adam lay awake until he heard his partner sink into dreamland. He worried that his dreams were full of drug dealers and violence, but that was one thing he could not alter. He mourned the death of Leo's carefree childhood. He mourned the death of his own purposeful adulthood – and swore he'd make amends.

Just before he fell to sleep Adam cleared his mind, looking at the ceiling of the Airstream – she drifted in and hovered just above him. Small tears formed in the corners of his eyes and he whispered soundlessly, "Justine."

The next day was like the first. They splashed in the surf, made boy-like meals, checked out all the functions of the trailer, and walked on the beach. They had no cares and no worries. Much of the time, Adam would piddle around the trailer while Leo hunted for sea glass. They had collected an unimaginable amount, Leo's eyes becoming trained to catch the glint of brown or green and the most coveted blue. They brainstormed about projects they could create with the sea glass. They always settled on finding the perfect clear glass bowl or cup to set prominently – proudly, on a mantel, window sill, or table. Adam said the kid could take them home but Leo wanted them to be in his mentor's home as a trophy.

On Sunday afternoon they loaded up and headed back to Santa Rosa. The exhilaration, the excitement had been used up. A palpable sadness hung in the air of the cab. Leo did not look back to see the following trailer; he did not utter again "it's gaining on us."

They put the Airstream to bed back in the weedy lot. The thing looked reborn: it was clean, it rested on new tires, and everything was in working order. But mostly it was pleased to be used, to assume its natural function – it was doing what it was born to do. It had achieved the goal so often missed by mortal beings – it had returned to Airstream paradise.

EIGHT – COURAGE

The next card read "Courage." This felt good to Adam. It showed a white flower, maybe a daisy, forcing itself up through a pile of rocks. A yellow glow surrounded the plant and faded into green. He looked at the reader, hopefully. She said, "I'm getting tired. You can read this one – what do you see?"

He looked closer at the card. "It takes courage to work through the difficulties of life. But, once you do, the feeling is light and worth the trouble."

She continued to look at him, waiting. He looked again, and then raised his head. "I will need courage for the difficulty ahead. It's not the reward – it's the work that matters."

The time with Leo at the beach had been transformative. Adam continued to meditate as he set up permanent quarters in the spare room. He and Cherie were ever more distant from each other. He would look at her waiting for a return glance, but she avoided eye contact. She puttered around the house and the garden and spent ever more time at work. To the outward eye she seemed content, assured. But he knew she was falling apart inside and thought the bottoming out might be explosive.

He tried not to think of Justine and never attempted to call; still he was sure he must make contact somehow. He often went back to the coffee house where they had met on the chance that she would apparate.

Adam was turning inside himself. He was less and less engaged at work, and entirely unmindful of it when he was not there. He looked forward to being fired, but knew in his heart he would have to take the step of quitting the job himself. The time was coming, and it was coming rapidly, and Adam felt it was closely connected to the dissolution of his marriage.

Cherie had brought home some good news recently about their debts and their net worth. He signed the form along with her that procured a new mortgage for the house combining the old one with the line of credit creating one smaller payment. Cherie scheduled an assessment and found that they had quite a bit of equity built up – should they sell today. Of course, Cherie watched the market – she said they would never sell in this market. And, why would they sell anyway? The house had every convenience they could want. Adam felt she was preparing to divide the assets just in case. It did not concern him.

Cherie was conscious that her husband was altering his life to suit himself, oblivious to the needs of the pair and especially oblivious to her. If she stopped to really reflect, she would admit that she did not want to end this union; but she worked hard to keep from being introspective. As Adam went more and more into himself, she went more and more into the world, staying busy.

Bud was a constant spokesman for the benefits of divorce. He would say, "Leave the bitch! Join the club, man – we'll have a party."

Adam was spending more time at Bud's than he was at home. He left his acoustic guitar in Bud's garage and started looking for a used electric that would better complement the electric bass. Whenever he could, Adam brought Leo with him.

There was little talk of taking the band on the road or even down to the tavern, which might have been problematic for Leo. They were happy within themselves – content to spend some hours in Bud's garage, which more and more resembled a music studio. They talked of getting recording equipment and laying down some tracks. Adam would sing the lyrics and the boys would keep the beat.

Sometimes Bud's woman would show up; she'd sometimes sing along and was always ready with praise. She paid special attention to Leo, full of congratulations and ready affection. It pleased Adam to see Leo's soulful interaction with a woman who was not drunk or indifferent.

One evening, after they had played for some weeks, Adam brought in some of his old tunes. He found Bud fiddling with an amplifier. "Hey, I've got something new to try.

Bud greeted him. "What-ya-got?"

"It's a blues riff, something I wrote back when I was in school. It's pretty good."

"Great, but you know I don't read. How's it go?"

"Let's get set up. I'll play through it and you can lay down some bass behind me. Leo can do a kind of slow soulful beat."

Bud looked around. "Hey, where's the kid?"

Adam responded, "He was right behind me," just as Leo hustled into the garage.

Bud said hello with a big bear hug that lifted Leo off the ground. Leo complained, "Easy man, don't you have a girl?"

Bud saw his opportunity. "Yeah, but she's not as pretty as you."

Adam broke up the party. "Get plugged in, Bud. Leo, we need a slower rhythm on this . . . it's blues."

Leo mumbled under his breath. "Oh great, this will cheer him up."

Bud picked up on the vibe. "Why, what's the problem."

Leo explained, "Just moping around . . . all the time."

Adam defended himself, "I'm not moping."

Leo finished the phrase. "He said . . . mope-a-lee."

Bud searched for a solution. "It's that lady isn't it? What's her name . . . Jezebel."

"Justine," Adam corrected him. "And it's nothing. Just chill it." He nodded to Leo, trying to get Bud to change the subject.

But Leo caught the gesture. "Yeah, the kid doesn't know anything."

Bud was still on track. "Just call her. It's not like you were doing her."

"Bud!" Adam was ready to throttle his friend.

"Okay, okay . . . let's electrify this mother. . . ."

"Bud!" Adam was pleading.

"I mean, let's play this nice number."

Adam started the piece on his guitar before anyone else could speak. Bud felt into the music for a minute, nodding his head with eyes closed, and then he started the bass line. This was new for Leo, so he waited cautious. When he felt the tempo somewhere deep inside himself, he started a soft drumming on the Cajon. They fell into an easy rhythm and flow.

It sounded good and the song sent Adam back in time to another rag-tag band playing in the old house on "The Hill" in Boulder, Colorado.

He remembered looking up from the fret board of his guitar and seeing Cherie in the doorway, a plastic cup in her hands, softly swaying to his song. It was the first time he had seen her, and he asked his roommate for her name. All he knew was that she was some hot sorority babe and sure to be a bitch. Adam agreed with the assessment, but made a point of catching up with her later that night.

Adam had a faraway look in his eyes as he brought the song to a melodious end. There was the slightest hint of wetness in his eyes and Leo noticed. "What's with you, Adam? Your dog die?"

Bud tried to help. "Guess it's not blues if it doesn't make you sad. Good job."

Adam regained some composure. "Let's wrap it up . . . school night."

Leo said, "Damn."

They finished putting the instruments to bed, and Adam sent Leo down to wait for him in the truck. Just as Adam was leaving the garage, Bud stopped him. "Let's get an early start tomorrow . . . what do you say?"

"I can't tomorrow. I'm going to be in town."

Bud questioned him. "Are you still hanging out at that coffee shop?"

"I don't know."

"Does she ever come in?"

"No."

"Then, what's the point?"

Adam explained that he had gotten used to hanging out there. He knew the barista behind the counter. He knew the guy that bussed the tables. People knew him by name now. "It feels like home."

"It feels like the last place you sat down with her. Friend, this is pathetic."

Adam was self critical. "You're right. It's pathetic. I'm a total loser. I'm done with that. I'm done with her. I'm never going back."

Bud patted him on the back. "There's the man."

On about the hundredth time Adam visited the coffee house, he took his usual seat with a good view of the door. He had given up the possibility of a chance encounter with Justine, but his visits here had become a habit. He found comfort in the place where they had set, conscious that her form had actually filled this space and he felt a remnant of her remained. He rarely looked at the door anymore.

He was engrossed in his book, the latest by Eckhart Tolle; and was deep in thought when he caught the slightest glimpse of her. She was at the counter ordering a coffee or some tea. Had she seen him already? Something squished in his heart. He looked up, straightened up, did not know what he would say or do. Would he run after her if she turned to leave, oblivious of him?

She took her tea in a real cup – not to go! His heart leaped. She turned into the room blowing steam off the top of the cup. She looked him in the eye as if she knew he had been there all along, as if she knew he had been in here for weeks. Neither moved and neither spoke. She took a sip of tea as if she was waiting. What in the hell was she waiting for?

He nodded his head to her as if to say, "What's up?"

She walked to "their" table, took a seat not looking at him, took another sip from the cup, got comfortable in her chair, then leveled her gaze to his face. He was visibly shaken, actually scared to death. She said, "Okay – you first."

He stumbled, opened his mouth, and nothing came out. He could not find words. Usually at times like this something else inside him would rush to his rescue – his ego? It covered for him when he did not want others to believe him dumb or lost for words. It could not cover for him now because it was gone. Where? Dissolved? Hiding some place dark, warm, and safe? He was unaccustomed to speaking from the heart unassisted. He waited for the words to come from this atrophied muscle, this heart. She was not impatient; she sipped her tea unperturbed.

"I've been spending time with Leo; lots of time. He's doing great – really great – you wouldn't believe it's the same guy."

She spoke and to him it sounded like angels whispering. "I know – he's great. That's why I wanted to talk to you."

Surprised, Adam said, "You wanted to talk to me?" He paused. "You could have just called."

"Why would I call when you're right here?" She was making fun of him.

He didn't mind and almost laughed. "We went camping – that was great. Doing these projects together – that's the secret, really. Tell everybody. And now we've got a little music thing going . . . made Leo a drum. He's amazing, I'm telling you, a natural. And he loves it – hanging out with me and my buddy. Not the best company for a teenager maybe – especially Bud – he's a little rough – but, jeez, they get along like brothers. Leo might be the older brother."

She laughed. She actually laughed. She also acted as if all this information was not news to her. She'd been talking to somebody.

She caught him in her brown eyes, over the top of her glasses. "You have to feel good about what you're doing. You saved his life. It's just unbelievable. But, there's something else I had to tell you. Celeste is out of jail. She's in a halfway house but they can only keep her a week or two. She's already clamoring to get her boy back, thinks that's what she needs to

stay sober. It's not. I'm trying to steer her into treatment –
thirty days minimum, ninety would be better – but she's
resisting. I see no substantive change in her – no change. She
hasn't reached her bottom yet; hard to believe. I'll tell you the
truth – when she hits bottom it will likely kill her. Just don't
want her taking Leo out with her."

Adam asked, "Does Leo know?"

"He knows. They've met – but that's all."

I'll have him over tonight. We'll hang out – maybe burn
some meat on the grill. I'll keep an eye on him."

"Good. Good." A deep breath out, closer to God, then,
"Well – I should probably go."

Adam reached for her and rested his hand on her arm.
"Don't go."

She hesitated. He spoke, "I don't want you to go. I don't
want anything else – I don't want anything from you – I just
don't want you to go."

They sat in silence for a while, sipping their drinks. Adam
felt that, familiar now, wetness in his eyes and blinked it away;
he still did not want to appear ridiculous. She pretended not to
see. Then she spoke, "This can't go anywhere."

He said, "I know. We could be friends, I think. Just see
each other sometimes to talk."

"Is that really what you want?"

"No, it's not what I want – I won't lie to you. It's what I'll
settle for. I don't think you know what I've been going
through."

"I don't know. It's not for me to know. It's your stuff – you'll work it out your own way."

"I don't need validation – I just wanted you to know I'm doing the work. I'm doing my meditation, I'm reading my books, I'm trying like hell to get out of my head. Jesus Christ, my head is going to be the death of me."

"So you're not done yet." She smiled.

He laughed. "Guess I could say I was done and you'd never know I wasn't."

He laughed again. "You'd never know."

At this point he was convinced she knew his every thought. He was convinced that deception was out of the question. Somehow he thought she held the keys to all the mysteries from all the yesterdays, to all of the tomorrows, especially to all of the todays. "Just another woman," his head told him, but his heart told him something else. He longed to look into her eyes, to lose his way again. He told himself this really was enough – to be in her company, to feel her presence, soak up all the essence he could, while he could. Yes, this is all he required; he lied.

They sat together, waiting out the remainder of the afternoon. He shared his life with her, careful not to ask her too much, careful not to promise anything. When their guard was down they had an easy way with each other. Adam wondered where the anxiety had gone. They laughed together. She wanted to know all about his journey inward and shared a little of her own careful not to show too much. It was agreed: they would meet again and talk – same place.

NINE – GOING WITH THE FLOW

Adam did not need to be told. He flipped the card and saw the color blue, the title: "Going With the Flow." That felt nice. The image was an indescript white figure afloat in a sea of swirling water: all blues and greens and a little gray. He thought for a minute the subject – he – could be drowning. The reader took her time. "You're right – but you will only drown if you resist. This is your future: going where the Divine has already made a place for you. It does not take effort – you cannot dive into this . . . you have to just let go. Don't hold on to the edge of the pool – you're not a baby. Let go. Let the current take you. If it drowns you, you will have a most happy death."

Adam brought Leo to his house as promised. They stood on the patio grilling pork chops, moving back and forth to the kitchen setting the table for their first family dinner that included the little woman. They were waiting for Cherie to show up. Wasn't he always just waiting for her to show up?

Adam gave Leo directions as he set the table. "Set out a wine glass for Cherie. She'll want some wine."

Leo said, "I might need some too."

"Funny."

They talked seriously about his future with his mom. Adam wanted to prepare him for the worst but didn't know how. They were already seated and passing around the food when Cherie came in. She was a little surprised to see the outcast boy at her fine French country table. She put her usual things away and joined them, a nice table setting before her. Leo filled her plate with the food they had prepared – he was a little afraid. Adam greeted her brightly like she was Ward Cleaver home for dinner with the family. Leo dished out the food while Adam filled her glass with a nice red wine. She drank.

"Some kind of occasion?" She queried.

Adam was bright and cheery. "Just happy to see you."

Cherie took a long drink from her glass. The 'boys' each had a glass of milk. Leo retired to the living room after dinner and watched a little mindless television.

Adam and Cherie cleared the dishes and met at the sink. Adam whispered to her the recent circumstances of Leo's situation.

"It's his mom, Celeste. She's out of jail and in a halfway house. She wants him back. I don't think he wants to go."

"You can't let him go back to that life . . . not after everything you've done."

"I'm watching out for him. And I'm starting him to work after school on my crew at the resort."

"What'd Phil say?"

"He doesn't know yet. It shouldn't be a big deal. Leo will work harder than all the others. He's a great kid."

Cherie spoke from a place of guilt. "I can see that. I wish I had been more help."

Adam took her hand. "You're here now."

Adam thought, "She really does have a good heart. Too bad it has to end."

At work the next day, Adam was more cheerful than usual. He removed himself from the office as much as possible. Phil wanted him to delegate everything, to stay glued to his phone and walkie-talkie, leaving only to try to catch somebody goofing off. But Phil could not hold him. He tooled around the grounds picking up trash with the high school kids, sweeping decks and cleaning grills with the crew.

He had brought Leo onto his crew at the resort now, over Phil's loud objections. "You hired Leo? You mean your little . . . whatever . . . the juvenile delinquent."

Adam defended, "He's a Little Brother, and a damn hard worker."

"It's nepotism . . . you're going to get us all in trouble. And, mark my words, this whole social experiment is going to blow up in your face."

Adam explained, "It's not nepotism. We're not really related. You'll be able to tell." He pointed to his own face. "You'll see . . . very little resemblance."

Nepotism was a joke. Phil had multiple family members working at the resort and pretended nobody knew. But, everybody knew. In the weeks to come, Leo became a star employee at the resort, even receiving an award from the managers. Phil re-imagined himself to have been his advocate from the beginning. Adam crept away from work early once a week to meet Justine at the coffee shop in town, and Leo was often on the job when he would see the Chevy pickup slip out the back entrance. He was just beginning to bond with Cherie now, so he was conflicted about being Adam's confidant.

Adam interacted very little with Leo on the job, choosing instead to let him learn to interact with the rest of the crew. He also needed no supervision. He did what he was told, and when he finished, he looked around for something else to do, without being told, much to the chagrin of his co-workers who were constantly being shown up.

On this day, Adam was walking past the front desk when the receptionist stopped him, hanging up the phone. "Adam, that was for you. Some woman named Justine. Said she's on her way over . . . will meet you in the parking lot."

Adam's heart jumped because she never called, leaving it to him to schedule the weekly meetings at the coffee shop. He knew it had to be about Leo. His mind was racing. There were too many worst case scenarios – and his mind entertained them all.

Adam asked the desk worker, "Is that all she said?"

"It sounded urgent. Who's Justine?"

He was distracted. "I don't know . . . a friend."

He saw her car enter the parking lot and he went to her. She got out and faced him showing worry, concern. "It's Celeste. She's dead. Found her OD'd on the steps of the halfway house. They took her to County General but it was too late. Don't know what she took; doesn't matter. They'll do an autopsy – they have to – to determine cause. Doesn't matter. It's done. You'll have to tell him. Is he here?"

Adam was overcome with sadness. "He's out back. I can get him. But give me a minute."

He didn't care about Celeste. She had done a cruel, selfish thing. At this moment he had only hate for her. Not for what she had done to herself, but what she had done to this child. And, for this horrible, thankless task that had been handed to him. Of course he would be the one to take this burden; there was nobody else. But, he would need a minute to prepare. He slouched against somebody's car. Justine looked at him – found his eyes – tried to give her strength to him. In the end, she could not help him.

Adam held the walkie-talkie to his mouth and pushed the button. "Leo, I need you in the office in one minute – over."

Justine heard Leo's response. "Roger, one minute – over." He sounded cheerful; he had no idea what he was approaching, sure that his Big Brother would send him to vacuum the lobby or some such thing. Justine could only look to Adam with deep sadness in her eyes. It was the first time she admitted to herself – she loved this man.

In the office Adam seated Leo with himself in the two chairs before his desk, then closed the door. Leo was confused, and sure he had done nothing wrong, quickly running through the events of the day in his mind.

Adam put his hand on his little brother's knee and looked him in the eye. "It's your mom. Somehow she got some pills, they found her at the halfway house, they took her to the hospital. It was too late."

Adam paused to let the news set in. It took a moment for Leo to add it up. His eyes filled with water and he raised his hand to his eyes. Then he was racked with deep, heavy sobs.

Adam held Leo's knees with both hands now, then helped him to his feet and held him tight with both arms. They had never been this close – both were a little stingy with affection. Now he let the little boy cry, his head on his shoulder. There was nothing in the world but those two. They would always have each other. Adam made the soundless promise – always, no matter what.

Justine had waited outside, but she accompanied the two of them to the car, her hand on Leo's shoulder. She blessed them and stepped aside. Adam left work without checking out with Phil, without giving instructions to his crew. They drove to Adam's home, Leo looking at the floor board, silent.

At the house, Adam set Leo in the living room. He gave him the TV remote and fixed him a sandwich and a soda which went untouched. Adam mostly left him to himself – sometimes coming in and sitting with the silent child. There was little said, there was little to say.

When Cherie came home, she was briefed quickly. Adam said, "We can put him on the couch – for now."

Cherie said, "No. We'll put him in my office. The day bed is comfortable. Give me a minute to move out my laptop and some papers."

Cherie stopped first to sit silently by Leo for a few minutes. She rested her hand on his shoulder, just holding space. When she stood to move into her office, Adam took her place. Leo was sullen and Adam felt helpless in providing solace. Cherie cleared off the desk in her office and put fresh linens on the daybed. Then, she returned to the living room to relieve Adam, who was desolate at his inability to remedy the situation. Cherie took her place, and held onto Leo's hand. He needed a woman's touch – she was available. Adam observed the pair from a distance; his heart full of love – for this, his wife.

Toward mealtime Adam made a move to lighten the air a little bit. While he fixed dinner, he asked Leo to set the table, to take out the trash – little things to keep him busy for a while. It felt right. The three of them sat down to salad and sautéed chicken breasts. Cherie and Adam made light conversation occasionally engaging Leo while he stared blankly at his untouched plate.

Cherie tried, "I'm getting some flowers to plant around the patio."

Adam responded, "Great . . . flowers. What are you getting?"

"More petunias. They grow fast and have good color. I'm thinking pink and blue. Maybe Leo could give me a hand."

Both adults looked at Leo expectantly, trying to create an opening with their eyes. Leo looked up at their persistent gaze and finally offered, "Sure."

In a strange way, Adam thought, it felt like family. Through all the hurt – because of the hurt, the despair – they had pulled together and made a family – if for just a little while.

TEN – INNER VOICE

The next card was filled with lots of blue, "Inner Voice."
There was a knowing feminine face with another woman's
head arising from the forehead, a woman wearing horns that
curved upward like the shape of a crescent moon. The forms
were setting on a flow of ocean with dolphins on either side.
The reader spoke up. "It's the High Priestess. She takes in
everything you offer and returns it to you in like form. She is
the Source."

"Everything you think, every action you take, will be
returned to you through her. Her participation is not optional.
It may be a blessing or a curse, but it is created only by you.
Every piece of your experience is a result of the reality you are
projecting. Every difficulty in your life has been placed there
by you. Nothing exists outside of the reality you have made
manifest – and it is all there to teach you. When you receive a
gift or blessing, know too that it is because you have made a
place for abundance to come to you."

Adam made arrangements, through Justine, to have Leo
move in with them. Cherie was entirely on-board, and seemed
to come alive in this nurturing role. The time he spent with
Leo meant less time with Justine. Their contact became
limited to phone calls full of knowing keywords and silences
that spoke volumes. They had a connection with each other
that transcended the need for words or physical contact.

Adam was somewhat confused though, about the emerging feelings he had for his wife. He saw her with new eyes and new appreciation. He began to see that he had created the space for her to appear cold and distant. He was sorry for the part he had played but was afraid to bring this to her. Sometimes he wondered if they should try again – if they should try. He wondered if it was ever enough just to love someone. Had they fallen away from each other for lack of love? He couldn't say, and these feelings of love and admiration were still covered over with a creeping sadness.

Taking over the parental role in Leo's life gave his life new meaning. He met with two of Leo's teachers when he got calls that the kid's grades had slipped. They understood the circumstances and really wanted to know what they could do to help. Leo went through the motions – going to school, doing chores – but Adam feared he was slipping away. He would sit alone in his new bedroom with books and homework spread out before him just staring at the desktop. He grudgingly accepted the specific help either Adam or Cherie would offer but there was a blankness to his gaze and little reaction to external stimuli.

Adam talked to the school psychologist about getting Leo some extra attention. He got a better response from Justine who offered to work with him herself. This was a great relief to Adam, who believed this woman held divine insight and mystical gifts of healing. Cherie was very worried about Leo, and did not hesitate when Justine was suggested as a gifted resource.

Cherie said, "Just because you have a thing for her, doesn't mean I don't want the best for Leo. You all think she can do miracles; let's give her a shot."

Adam responded, "I don't have a thing . . . she's just become a good friend. I can't help it she's a woman."

Cherie was grateful to Justine for her ability to get the courts to place Leo with them temporarily. Adam was working on getting permanent custody and Justine was his primary counselor. He said, "She has a way."

Cherie quipped, "I'll bet she does."

They both greeted Leo when he trudged into the living room bleary eyed from sleeping too long. Adam commented on his bed-head, trying to illicit a response. Leo grunted and flipped on the cartoon network. Badger nudged his thigh, and Leo petted the dog absently, focused on Sponge Bob.

Cherie gave Adam directions. "See if you can get him to eat some cereal."

"I can't believe you got him that sugar cereal."

"He's a teenager. Isn't that what they eat? I just don't want him to fade away on our watch. When he starts eating again . . . then, we'll know."

Cherie was in the garden when Justine arrived to take Leo for a short drive and a walk in the park. Adam met her on the front porch, giving her arm a light touch. Adam wanted to steal a moment of her time before he gave her over to Leo.

He said, "God, it's so good to see you. It's been great talking to you on the phone, but I really miss our sitting down together."

"You've had your hands full. Where's Leo?"

"He's in the living room . . . Cherie's around back. I just wanted a minute . . . I think I might need your help as much as Leo does."

She took a step back. "I'm not going to be much help to you."

"What do you mean?"

"I'm leaving. I told you I was leaving. I've stayed too long. I wanted to get things squared away for Leo, but now there's nothing to keep me here."

Adam felt like he was sinking fast. "What about us?"

"Adam, there is no us. Don't create a fantasy about us. You can't know why we might have a connection. I might exist in your awareness just to help you and Leo get together."

"That alone is like a . . . miracle. But, that can't be all. Where are you going?"

"I've taken a position . . . in Sedona. It's counseling with a great group of healers. It's a holistic center: body work, breath work . . . me."

Adam tried to gather his wits. He tried to put himself in her place, but struggled. "Of course you have to do this. It's just so sudden."

"It's not sudden for me. It's been coming a long time. It's not personal; it's my stuff and I need to attend to it. This will give you a chance to stand on your own; you don't need to lean on me. Maybe there's a chance you can reconcile with your wife."

"I know it looks like I'm not taking care of that. I've been paralyzed – I don't know why. But, the end is coming. I feel like it needs to unfold in its own way, in its own time. Isn't that what you say?"

Justine agreed, "That's what I say. Now, I'm taking myself out of the picture. This is a piece of the unfolding you have to accept."

He wasn't finished explaining. "I feel like I need to consider what's best for Leo. This thing with Cherie will resolve – we both know the truth. I just want to do it right, with respect . . . with love? Does that make sense?"

"It makes perfect sense. Don't you see? This is perfect timing, this is divine timing. I should not be here – I've known it for awhile. Now I'm paying attention."

"I can deal with this but my head is screaming for some explanation, some definition. I don't even know what we are – this thing – we are. I know you don't want to name it."

"I can't name it anymore than you can – all I can do is let it be. I don't know what it is – I don't know what it will be."

"This is too hard for me. I've never been conscious with somebody – a woman, you, before. God-damn-it, I don't know how to do this."

"I don't know how to do this either. Just let it be."

"I will, I will. I just want to know what it is I'm supposed to let be."

Adam was near tears. Justine placed a hand on his arm and she kissed him on the cheek. She was kissing him goodbye.

When he brought her into the house, Cherie was coming in from the patio, peeling off her gardening gloves. Adam said, "Cherie, I want you to meet Justine."

Cherie extended her hand politely and Justine held on to her for just a little too long than was comfortable. They looked at each other, Justine wanting to know the heart of this woman who had been companion to her friend for thirty years. Cherie was conscious of her husband's affection for this woman, though nothing was ever spoken. She thought, "Women know these things." She thought, "We both know what the other is thinking." But it all went unsaid.

Cherie was wary of this soul who seemed to have captivated her husband's attention. Cherie made the quick assessment that she herself was somewhat prettier and certainly younger. Adam used to call her his trophy wife – she liked that – though those words were no longer spoken. Cherie was grateful to have this woman's help with Leo. But, she was also cautious of this . . . her rival?

Justine broke the spell. "I have wanted to meet you for some time. I know you are a great support for Leo."

Cherie was afraid her own motherly instincts might have atrophied for lack of usage. "I've tried to help him, but I'm not a professional. Adam always says we don't know what in the hell we're doing."

Adam spoke, "She's great with Leo. You should see them together."

"You have both been a lifeline for him." Justine wanted to assure this woman of her value and her key role in the child's well-being. "He's mourning the loss of his mother and the loss of his own childhood. His whole world is turned upside down, no matter how much he loves the two of you. He needs to grieve but he can't stay there. Some people get stuck. It's best to let it be, and then release it. It will come up again, but next time he'll know how to process."

Cherie was encouraged. "I guess they're right about you. I'll get Leo. He's expecting to have a drive."

Justine added, "It's a beautiful day for a drive. We'll talk and maybe get some lunch. It'll be fun."

Adam saw the pair out of the driveway, and then joined Cherie in the backyard. She was repotting some patio plants, and he helped her with the heavy lifting. They worked side by side without speaking. Adam was thinking about Justine's imminent departure and Cherie was trying not to think. He broke the silence. "I'm thinking it's time for another camping trip."

"With you and Leo."

"Yes, with me and Leo." He was wondering who else he might go camping with.

"Good idea. That will be good for him. Nice we're finally getting some use out of the Airstream."

"Yeah, it feels good to have it out of mothballs. It's like it's living its life's purpose."

Cherie reminisced, "I remember we had some big plans."

"Oh yeah, we were going to get back to Colorado, but soften the camping experience for you a little. God, you remember those coyotes?"

"That would be the last time I went camping."

"I know you didn't like that part, but there was something magic about that night. Do you remember the stars?"

"I remember the stars, but I mostly remember the critters."

Adam chuckled, remembering. "You didn't like it that I found so much humor in the situation."

"When I had to go to the bathroom."

"And you had to have an escort."

"We were surrounded by wolves, and I had to go."

"They weren't wolves. But I protected you."

"It was humiliating."

"It might sound weird, but I felt very close to you."

Now, Cherie laughed. "Because you were close to me – while I squatted to pee. And the wolves were closing in; I've never been so scared."

"But then we returned to the safety of a little nylon tent."

"Which is exactly why we got the Airstream."

"And never used it." Adam started cleaning off the tools.

Cherie paused, feeling how to say it. "Maybe it's time."

Adam did not understand. "What . . . for you . . . to camp?"

"Technically, I bought it. It was for me. I guess you forgot."

Adam was confused by this sudden turn. "I know you found it. It was all your idea. I just thought you lost interest."

"Well, now I'm interested. Why should you guys have all the fun?"

"You think it would be fun?"

Justine's visit with Leo was productive. He opened up with her and seemed to start to settle back into himself again. He had been floating, held in the flow of sadness and despair, and had risked being dragged into the swift water to drown. She gave him a place to stand, a way to slip away from the rapids and hang onto some temporary refuge until he could move again into a flow that would not drag him down. She was his rock. Adam loved the metaphor. He had called her that often, even laughing about how hard he leaned on her. She was petite – just a little thing – and he feared all the support she lent would use her up, wear her down.

Now Justine was going away and he would have to learn how to stand on his own. He had a flash of understanding: this was exactly why she had to move out of his awareness. He had hoped to somehow be of service to her and now felt cheated out of that opportunity. He wanted to be her rock, but saw now that he was meant to pass it on. He was to be Leo's rock. Justine had showed him how.

At dinner Leo actually dug into his chicken and rice. Adam and Cherie were delighted to see the change and continued their discussion about an Airstream excursion.

Leo said, "She really wants to go camping."

Cherie reminded him, "Hey, I'm right here."

He redirected his question to her. "I mean . . . you . . . really want to go?"

Leo had not seen this aspect of her before, and frankly neither had Adam for at least a couple decades.

Cherie looked at Adam. "That was the original idea."

Adam said, "Yes – but I thought you lost interest a long time ago. I know it's like a little house – but it's still going out in the woods where, you know, stuff is crawling around."

Cherie explained, "I like the outdoors. I'm not a wimp – remember, we used to go camping."

"I remember. . . ." Adam thought of a life-line: "Maybe we should all go."

Leo tried to help but he was also conscious of his foster parent's sleeping arrangement as well as their simmering displeasure with each other. "Yeah, sure . . . we can all go. You know . . . there's only two beds."

Leo let the statement sink in for a minute and the two adults tried not to make eye contact. Adam took another bite of chicken. "What in the hell was she thinking." And Cherie took a long drink of wine.

Suddenly Leo had a brainstorm. "I know! The two of you should go. That would be cool with me. Maybe you guys could use some time . . . together."

Adam reacted, "There's no way I'm leaving you alone."

"You think I've never been home alone. I'm not a child."

Adam was inflexible. "I don't care what you are. On my watch, you are not going to be left alone."

Leo had a brilliant idea. "I know. I'll stay with Bud!"

And Adam countered, "That might be worse than being alone."

Leo pleaded, "Come on. . . ."

Adam and Cherie finally made eye contact, he paused, "You sure you want to do this?"

Cherie was flip. "What the hell. It's my turn, isn't it?"

Adam was searching for someplace to stand; his mind was spinning. "Okay, if you want to go . . . we should be able to find some who won't corrupt the kid."

Leo reminded them, "I ain't no kid."

Adam remembered, "Yeah I know, you ain't no kid."

Adam's head was swirling – he did not know what this meant and did not know how to navigate this water. Why had he placed this into his awareness – what was he to learn?

Justine was already on her way to Arizona and he was only able to reach her occasionally on her cell phone. When he relayed this latest story to Justine she only responded, "Oh." It's not like they were dating or anything. Why did he think he was cheating on Justine? He was married to Cherie, wasn't he?

Over the next few days Cherie planned the camping trip like it was a four star vacation. They would camp outside of the town of Mendocino, an artsy village just to the north that was known for its many shops, and breathtaking views of the rugged coastline. She stocked the Airstream with some fine Sonoma wines and upgraded the bed linens and towels. The wine glasses in the overhead bin were real crystal. She hung a fluffy robe in the small closet. She was not planning on roughing it.

It felt strange to have Cherie next to him in the pickup instead of Leo. Besides, she was rarely seen on the road outside of her Lexus. She seemed to be opening and this only served to make him more confused. She acted genuinely happy as they headed toward Mendocino. The campground was north of town with full hook-ups and just a short walk to a hidden beach. There would be shallows to explore and local surfers in the water. They had not discussed the sleeping arrangements.

Cherie was like a little girl. "We haven't been to Mendocino in so long. We can go shopping and there are nice restaurants."

Adam added, "Just like in the National Forest."

"But no squatting in the woods. I'm going to miss that."

"Me too."

She was satisfied with herself. "It's my idea of camping; really roughing it. We've got dinner reservations at seven." She looked at her watch.

"I could have cooked."

She said, "Don't be silly. It's Café Beaujolais; you'll love it."

Once they reached the campground, Cherie helped as much as she could to set up. Adam made up the single bed before they drove to town for dinner. Adam noticed that Cherie was a little overdressed for camping. He likewise noticed that he was a little underdressed for Café Beaujolais. They each let the other be.

Adam and Cherie sat in the café and had a sumptuous dinner; not a hot dog in sight. There was candlelight and they split a bottle of wine. Now that they had Leo in common there was no end of discussion where he was concerned. After dinner they walked around town, adding some fresh air and time to their pleasant wine buzz. Most of the shops were already closed, so they looked in the windows.

Cherie saw some hand thrown dinner plates she had to have. "At least four." And there was a hand-painted lazy Susan for the dining room table she wanted. She said, "This is great. We'll know just where to go when we come back."

As the fog started rolling in, blanketing the town, Cherie pulled the collar of her jacket closer around her neck. Adam said, "It's getting cold. We should head back."

As they trudged through the fog in silence, Cherie's hand innocently bounced against his. Without looking up, without speaking, she took his hand. Surprised, he responded instinctively, taking a better grip. They did not exchange a glance – drifting through the fog, hand in hand. It was like they were in love again. At the pickup they let go and he let her in the passenger side before moving around to the driver's door.

Back at the trailer they both made busy getting ready for bed, taking turns in the tiny bathroom. He had set his stuff on the twin bed and hers on the double bed up front. When she came out of the bathroom in her robe, he pretended to be busy straightening the cabin. Halfway down the aisle way she caught his eye and said, "You don't have to sleep back here."

He said, "It's not bad – Leo sleeps here."

"Come up front," She said it and moved toward the larger bed.

"You know it's only a full."

She said, "I know".

She removed her robe – she was wearing a silky white gown. The garment showed the curve of her hips and the shape of her breasts. Something stirred in him. She got into bed, moving to the far side to make room for him beside her. He hesitated, confused.

She flipped out the light beside the bed and slid down between the sheets. He moved to the side of the bed and waited a moment. The only light was from the moon shining through the open skylights. The air was chilled and there was the faint smell of the ocean. He slipped in beside her and they held each other, wordlessly.

It was the first time they had made love in months – he had stopped counting. It was the last time they would ever make love.

Cherie sat up in bed after Adam had fallen into peaceful slumber. She held the quilt up to her neck to ward off the seaside chill, and she surveyed her surroundings. The interior of the trailer was cozy and cave-like. She peeked through the new hung curtains and saw the grass was wet with dew. The campground was asleep; there was no movement.

She felt a deep sense of peace as she closed the curtain and looked down at Adam like she was seeing him for the first time. She let the thought rise in her awareness that they had struggled and suffered so much over the last many years.

Cherie thought that much of their suffering had been needless; many of the hardships had been imagined and existed only in their thoughts. That was his big new thing: moving out of thinking. She was skeptical, but she admired him for trying . . . or, what did he say? "Trying not to try." She unfocused her eyes and sank into the bluish haze that seemed to gather around the bed. She noticed the moon glow streaming in through the skylight; a clearly defined moonbeam. She raised her hand, palm up, to intercept the beam; and gazed dreamily for moments at her illuminated hand.

The weekend was pleasant, even enjoyable. They did not pretend to be some past incarnation of themselves; it was more like spending time with a pleasant stranger, someone you didn't know but were related to. On the ride home, they chatted and listened to music. Adam thought this must have been some sort of ceremony for saying goodbye. Had they made some peace with each other, some . . . closure?

ELEVEN – THE TOWER CARD

*The dark reader motioned for Adam to turn the next card.
It was "The Tower". She did not make a sound or change
expression. In this deck, the Tower was a cross-legged figure
in a pose for meditation. Lightning bolts were streaming from
the heavens, landing on the figure's head and shoulders. Fire
arose from all the chakras, from the groin to the top of the
head, and two naked figures were seen being thrown from the
tower to their imminent destruction. She said, "It is the end of
everything – in the world of form."*

*He didn't know from where the understanding came. He
tried to see her face and asked, "Will I lose everything?"*

*She said, "You will want to. It's a clearing of the field.
You will be able to see for a long distance, finally being
unobstructed. You will have no restrictions. You will have
nothing. This is your fondest wish – your deepest desire: to
start again."*

He said, "You think I want to lose everything?"

*"The part of you that knows the truth needs to be revealed
now. This is the only part of you that is eternal . . . and
fearless."*

*He was quiet. He felt the earth shift slightly beneath him .
. . somewhere underground . . . a subtle movement . . .
somewhere beyond his senses . . . somewhere beyond reason.
He knew this was the point of the reading, but he did not know
if the visit was over.*

The reader had one more thought. She said, "Step into your truth; the one who watches the fearful man. That is the one that needs to emerge. Everything else will fall away. There is no rebirth without a little dying."

Adam heard a distant roll of thunder as a cloud moved over the sun, darkening the plaza. He looked up at the sky like he was expecting something to be revealed.

Adam was grateful to be home. He did not like to be away from Leo. He and Cherie settled back into their separate bedrooms, living amicably separate lives. He longed to be in conversation again with Justine but felt terribly conflicted and did not know what to say to her.

When he finally reached her on the phone, he was resolved to keep the details of the camping trip to himself. But part of him still believed she could read his every thought, that she at least would sense a "disruption in the force."

He told Justine, "I feel like something is about to happen – but I don't know what it is."

Justine answered, "Nothing is about to happen – it has – it is already happening.

There is nothing worse than thinking you are right on the edge of something, especially right on the edge of receiving. You have to believe it has already happened – you have already received it."

Adam was still and waited for understanding. He knew he could not wrap his brain around it; the brain was of no use at all.

Over the following weeks, Cherie observed her husband pulling away from her more and more. There was a moment just after the camping trip that she thought there might be a way through for the two of them. But it unsettled her to realize that he was grieving over Justine's moving away. She saw him continue his meditation and his study. He was cheerful with Leo and anxious to be away from home, playing in Bud's garage. He was friendly in his interactions with Cherie, but there was something else she sensed. A light had gone out in his eyes. He seemed to have come completely unattached from her. There was no attraction; there was no desire.

When Cherie initiated the divorce proceedings, Adam was relieved but self damning about his own lack of initiative in the matter. Adam did not understand why he could not have taken the lead. He felt the urgency to be moving on, into the flow, yet he could not easily release his hold on the last thirty years.

He had been paralyzed. When she broke the news to him there was no discussion; he shook his head in agreement, overtaken by grief. It made him feel a little stupid that it was she who took charge of this incidental. His ego would have liked it better if he had taken charge, but there was no upper hand here to be had. There were no winners. No, he thought, there are only losers.

She already had a lawyer – a woman – here in town. Nothing contested, everything down the middle, she kept her debt, he kept his. It fit the pattern. He thought he was the stronger one – maybe the wiser one, maybe even the smarter one. But, it was always she who took charge, who made things happen who could operate with ease in the world of form as if she belonged there.

Adam wanted at least to bring her into some kind of awakening, some kind of other consciousness that would free her from the world. But, he could not save her. She would manage her own redemption and it would occur exactly where, when, and how it was supposed to. She was on her own path and he could not drag her onto his; he now saw the error of even wishing he could.

They stayed in their separate corners of the house, Leo somewhere in limbo, Badger gravitating to the attentive boy. Adam worked with social services to get sole custody, but everything was harder now that Justine was gone. *Everything* was harder. He managed to get things done and he managed to stand upright, but a light had gone out in the world. He was grieving the end of his marriage and he was sick over the absence of the one he loved. He knew he was not much help to Leo as he managed the details of separating entirely from his former life, but the kid was resilient and seemed to be making his own way.

Leo was mourning too. Although he wanted to be with Adam, he had become quite close with Cherie. She visited with him daily, pumping him for information about school, his classes, his teachers, his friends . . . any girlfriends? They had developed an easy rhythm with each other, helping each other to heal, and Adam hated to see that end.

Cherie wanted to keep the house; that was alright with Adam. When she said she would buy his share of the equity, he told her she could keep it. This surprised her but it felt just right to him. It was her house; to him it was just a pile of sticks. When he was gone and it was out of his eyesight, it would cease to exist. She still needed the house, he did not.

To Adam, the only other thing of value between them was the dog. Cherie took the high road. "He's your dog – you should have him."

He appreciated the offer but convinced her that Badger should stay with her. She would be the one who would be entirely alone in spite of her friends, clients, and associates. He felt some guilt for this, and knew it would be greedy to take this pet away even though Badger was aging and would not be much longer for this life. Cherie had been a reluctant dog owner but once that barrier had been broken, she had developed a heart-felt attachment. She would have her companion; Badger would greet her every morning and every evening after work like she was the center of his universe. She was. Badger would have the yard and someone to love. They would have each other.

When Adam gave his notice at the resort, Phil fired him on the spot.

Adam said, "You're kidding me. I'm offering you two weeks."

Phil was absolute. "Two weeks ain't shit. Go ahead, clear out your desk. And don't take any pens or paper clips. I'll give you twenty minutes."

"I'm offering to help you with the transition."

"I don't need you. I never did."

"I just can't believe you would be that stupid. You're cutting your own throat. You'll have to do my job and yours."

Phil was angry and wanted to hurt Adam more than he wanted to save himself pain and anguish. "I could do your job with all my hands and feet tied behind my back. I'm serious about calling the police."

All Adam could say was, "Okay . . . it's you circus . . . I mean thanks . . . really, Phil. I want you to be well."

Phil looked at him, incredulous. "You're down to about fifteen minutes." He looked at his watch.

Adam walked over to the CD player on a side table and slid out the disc. He picked up his briefcase and held up the CD so Phil could see it. "John Williams, classical guitar. It's pretty good."

Phil did not respond but took another look at his watch. Adam set the CD in a pocket of his briefcase and left the building. He wanted to say goodbye to his crew but that option had been taken away. At his pickup, he scanned the parking lot and observed Antonio at the far end stepping off a golf cart. When their eyes connected, Adam raised his hands, palms up, and shrugged his shoulders. Antonio returned the gesture with a confused look of wonder. Adam laughed to himself, climbed into the truck and drove off the property.

Adam knew this day would become company legend and the guys would get a good laugh out of it. That was the best he could leave them. They were on their own, adrift in the world of Phil. He would miss them. In spite of the intolerable conditions, they had reached some agreement, some equilibrium with each other.

They had taught him to not take his life or his work so seriously. They had taught him more than he had ever taught them. Though now he knew there would be no one to shelter them, to protect them from "the man." He dreamed that Phil would miraculously heal and find his true calling.

He dreamed. This was the kind of dreaming that was constructive. He was imagining a better Phil, a better world. It was the best he could do. And Adam could not be happier with the turn of events. Now he would have more time to attend to the move and to wrap up the details of taking his ward out of the state.

TWELVE – TRAVELING

He flipped the next card: "Traveling." It showed a lonely figure on a high mountain path, mist rising from the valleys, a golden sun straight ahead. He thought the sun must be rising – that's more hopeful than setting – and it had not yet burned the morning fog away.

When school was out in the spring, Adam and Leo pulled the Airstream over to the house and started loading up all they would need for the last leg of their journey. Cherie assisted them, giving up some nice plates and bowls which Adam objected to receiving.

"We're camping – we could eat off metal plates."

"You should have something nice even if you're sitting on a log. Besides, it's the Longaberger from you sister – you should have it."

Adam hated the idea of sharing the news of the divorce with his sisters. He called the one with whom he confided. He trusted Marie to disseminate the news to the rest of the family. Marie had been the one who consoled him over the years. She knew he was lost and that somehow he would need to make a drastic change. He had not begun to tell his friends the news. He dreaded the inevitable questions and obligatory words of comfort and consolation. He seriously contemplated sending a generic mass e-mail that would rip off the band-aid quickly.

Adam suddenly understood that this was part of what kept him in the marriage. He did not want to admit his failure as a mate, as a husband. But, that was the truth – he was an utter failure at maintaining this relationship. He had been failing at it for many years and could not even admit it to himself. Moving past this would be liberating, and any future relationship would be a test. He resolved to be free of all the demons of the past.

When Adam told Cherie that Bud was coming over to help prep the trailer she said, "I'll lock up the liquor."

Adam thought that was a good idea. "I wanted to warn you about something. He thinks you're fair game now that you and I are . . . you know. . . ."

Cherie volunteered, "Not dating?"

"Exactly. He's always had a crush on you. I wasn't sure you noticed."

"I noticed, but maybe you could let him know . . . he's dreaming!" She pointed to herself. "This is way out of his league. Besides I don't think there's going to be much dating. I don't think I should be with anyone."

"I don't want you to say that. I want you to find happiness with somebody. I don't want to hear the details, but I want you to be happy."

"I'm thinking that being happy might mean being alone for awhile, maybe longer than awhile. I've never really been by myself; most people have. I think I need that. I think it's time."

Adam corrected himself, "I keep forgetting that what is right for me, might not be right for everybody. You know best. You know your own heart."

"So you're still looking for love? I'll bet you rebound right back into some crappy relationship."

"I plan to be careful. But I want to love someone and to be loved."

"Because you didn't have that with me?"

"I think we had that once. I don't know what happened. It went away, and thinking it might come back kept me here too long."

The conversation was over so Cherie changed the subject noticing that Badger was setting in the cab of pickup while the boys loaded up the trailer. "He thinks you're going to leave him here."

Adam corrected, "He thinks we're both going to leave."

"He's used to being fed by you. You're the one who takes him to the vet."

"Maybe when you start taking him to the vet Badger won't favor you so much."

"He doesn't favor me. He just prefers women."

"I wanted him to be my dog. But from day one, he liked you best. Every night he ends up at your feet. He's your dog." Adam nodded his head toward Leo who was eavesdropping on the conversation. "Besides, I get the kid."

Leo piped in, "Thanks a lot."

Adam said, "No trouble. We flipped a coin."

Leo made a joke. "Who won?"

When Bud arrived, they made some last minute adjustments to the trailer, checking the electric, the suspension, the brakes. Leo was boiling with excitement. Cherie loaded all the CDs she wanted on her IPod leaving the bulky dinosaurs to Adam who, to Leo's disbelief, didn't even own an IPod, thinking it might be just a fad.

There was a palpable sadness in the air around the division of property. This was eased in part by the fact that Adam had no plans for life after the Airstream. He wanted to see where it took him, and said he would come back for a few things when they got settled. Cherie kept bringing things from the house and he kept sending them back. They were already overloaded for simple camping. They made a place of honor in the cab for Adam's guitars and Leo's drum.

While Bud rummaged around the mechanics of the trailer and the pickup, Cherie brought out the glass globe filled with sea glass from the camping trip. She handed it to Leo delicately, like it was a crown jewel. "I don't want you to forget this; it was on the mantle."

Leo gazed at the mass of polished glass holding it up to the sunlight. He lowered the globe to his lap contemplating it for a few moments, and then he handed it back to Cherie. "I want you to have it."

Cherie protested, "No, it's too much. It's a treasure. It won't take up any room in the truck. Take it with you."

Leo was firm. "I don't have anything else that is mine to give you. I want to . . . I need to give you something. So you'll remember. . . ."

Cherie took a quick step forward and hugged Leo hard around the neck. "I'll remember. I don't need anything to help me remember." She stepped back with tears in her eyes and pressed her hand to her heart. "I have you here . . . I'll always remember."

Leo had pressed the globe into her hands during the embrace, and now blinking back tears Cherie sorted through the glass pieces and retrieved a large blue one that resembled an amoeba. She said, "I will accept the gift, but take this one. Keep it in your pocket. It will bring you something." She whispered to him, "It has special powers. Touch it when you need strength . . . or truth."

Leo took the blue glass carefully and examined it. Cherie's crying triggered the release of his own tears, and he told her, "I'll keep it in my pocket. When I touch it, I'll think of you. You will give me strength."

Bud and Adam where witness to this exchange and stared at them now in stunned silence. When they came to their senses they quickly busied themselves with the packing of the truck, aware that they had been privy to something private, intimate, and sacred.

When it was time to say goodbye to Bud, Adam told him, "You can pop out to Sedona any time. We're going to keep the music going. If you show up, you're in the band."

"I've got my business here. I can't just pack up and leave."

Adam consoled him. "You don't have to relocate. Just show up; we'll make a place for you."

"How are you going to start a band if you're living in a trailer park?"

"I don't know. We'll improvise. That small town is full of creative people, and I figure they're just waiting for us to show up. We'll make ourselves available." Adam redirected himself to Leo. "Isn't that right?"

Leo answered, "That's right boss. The way I see it: Sedona is waiting for us, and they don't really know what to do next . . . until we arrive."

Adam spoke proudly, "You see, that's the kind of talk that makes things happen."

Bud had another piece of advice for his friend. "I want you to take a good long look at that box drum . . . that cajon. There's something there. I don't know what it is. It's innovative and fun. Just look at it . . . that's all I know."

"Okay, we'll look at it. Now, get out of here before we all start crying."

Bud and Adam embraced each other, both choking back tears but were mostly successful. But Bud completely lost it when he went to hug Leo goodbye. Leo tried to mitigate the big man's big tears by joking. "He's killing me! I've got broken ribs . . . I'm not kidding."

They all laughed as Bud started for his truck. He started to stop to give Adam one more goodbye, but thinking better of it hopped into the cab just as Cherie was coming out of the house. She had words of comfort for him. "Don't worry, Bud. I'll be here. We'll have each other."

These words of hope completely transformed Bud's composure. He put on a big smile and spoke to Adam. "Don't you worry about Cherie . . . I'll take good care of her."

Bud drove away, and Adam offered, "You don't want to toy with the big guy."

"Thought I could at least throw him a bone. Besides, who knows. . .? I've got dinner on the patio. You need to take a break."

Adam and Leo and Cherie went in for their last supper – their last time together as a family. These last days with Cherie had been surreal. He wondered if they would have ended this way had they been this genuine all along. If they had been that true, they probably would have never ended up together anyway. They had been drawn together by their individual neediness and if they had not been needy, they might not have found each other. Still, she was generous and noble as she shooed him out of her house, out of her life.

They would have one more night in the Santa Rosa suburb, and over a hearty meal they all promised they would get together again as a family, if only for a little while. Badger hovered around the table begging for a hand-out, gravitating to Leo, who was the easiest mark. Adam thoughts drifted off, over the miles, through the desert and down the mountain to Sedona. The bed of the truck was over loaded; they would need to rent a storage space when they landed, wherever they landed. Adam knew he was bringing himself, the Airstream, and Leo to Sedona. He did not know what Sedona would bring to him.

He had an address for Justine but hated the short conversations they had on the phone. He had always been indifferent about telephones and disliked e-mail even more. He felt it was hard enough to connect with another person without that contact being mediated – channeled through tiny wires or satellite signals. Justine had promised nothing and Adam tried his best to not hang fantasies on what might be. She kept saying it was right to honor their connection without becoming "attached". To Adam it felt like a contradiction.

He had made these mistakes before. He knew now that he had made a dream in his mind about the couple called "Adam and Cherie" and he had tried to live that dream. Now he was mourning not the loss of the marriage but the loss of the marriage he had imagined but had never been realized. Mourning the loss of a fantasy is literally mourning the loss of nothing at all. He kept reminding himself and still it felt like something real.

The next morning, the truck and trailer were fully loaded and gassed up, with every last minute object put aboard. Leo said goodbye to his temporary mother then waited in the cab. This parting held a heavy feeling of finality and Adam did not want to stretch it out.

He said, "Okay. Don't worry about us. I'll call you when we get there . . . let you know we're not dead. And, I'll be back you know, to get some stuff."

Cherie said, "Okay, I'll take care of your stuff."

"I want to say . . . ," he stuttered. "I want to say . . . I'm just sorry for everything. I wish we could have made it work –

you know, we can't. It's not your fault – it's nobody's fault. I made so many mistakes. I can see that now. I want you to know . . . I'm sorry."

Near tears, Cherie made her confession, "It wasn't you. You think I don't know what people say about me? I know I'm hard to live with. I don't think anyone else would have lasted so long. You stuck it out . . . you did your best. I'll always be grateful for that."

They were both crying but Adam managed to say, "I have to say this. It was always you who took care of the details. You always made the hard decisions and I always went along. Maybe I shouldn't have. But letting me go . . . that's the greatest kindness you could have given me. And I want you to know . . . I noticed."

Cherie was crying uncontrollably and could only say, "It's alright. We'll be alright."

He bent down and kissed her lightly on the lips. She let him. He stepped into the truck and drove away. Cherie stood in the driveway with her hand in the air, tears streaming down her face. When the truck pulled out of sight, she composed herself and bent down to rub Badger on the head. She went back into the house, her dog following at her heels.

The pickup rumbled through town, the Airstream just behind, following and sometimes gaining on them. Adam was still tearing up as they drove away, and Leo let him be, trying to dampen his own sense of enthusiasm.

Adam flashed back to the first time he had kissed Cherie. He had known her for awhile at school but they had never dated. They had just made arrangements to have dinner downtown when he ran into her between classes at the Memorial Union. He was running out as she was running in. They talked hurriedly, making last minute arrangements for the date. She was bundled up against the cold and he loved the redness the wind had left upon her cheeks. Before he turned to leave, he leaned down to kiss her on the lips – she let him. He knew that he was kissing her hello. Now after all this time the kiss was for goodbye.

The interstate rolled beneath them as they took the trek around the San Francisco. It was always a tricky venture pulling a trailer behind: multiple lane changes, sudden traffic jams, and even a toll booth where they had to pay for every axle. But they were carefree – stopping for sodas and chips to munch, abandoning every thought of healthy living. Adam reminded Leo that this was their last chance for reckless living. In Sedona he would have to get used to all raw food, daily yoga, and rigorous hikes into the red rocks. Leo said that was just fine.

They had an RV park in mind for the end of their first day halfway down Interstate-5. Just before they got there, they smelled the feed-lot at Harris Ranch, well before they passed it. Leo was dismayed; he was anything but vegan and could have lived on burgers, but the sight was truly upsetting.

He said, "Jesus Christ, they're standing all day in their own shit! That's inhumane!"

This was not Adam's first look at, or smell of a feedlot, but he could not defend it. "Yes, that's what they call it."

The smell and image haunted Leo as they set up camp at the park. Adam asked him, "Do you want to let them out?"

He was kidding, but Leo was serious. "Yes – we'll let them out."

"We can't let them out."

"Why not? We're in the middle of nowhere. We just sneak up there and open the gate."

Adam was laughing. "We can't let them out. It's a big operation . . . they probably have security. The gates are sure to be locked."

Leo glared at him and he relented. "Okay, we'll let them out. We'll have dinner and wait until dark, then we'll go let them out."

This lifted Leo's mood and they sat down to a nice salad out of the trailer fridge and turkey sandwiches; Adam thought better of grilling up the burgers he had planned.

It was dark when they finished dinner. They stepped into the unhitched pickup, kidding each other about wearing dark clothes, and Leo joking about Adam darkening his face. They pulled up past the ranch restaurant and hotel complex looking for a frontage road that would take them to the feedlot. Adam was sure there would at least be security cameras, but they found a gate fronting the lot and no sign of any guard. They stepped out of the truck looking around like they were in a movie and still there were no guards.

They reached the fence and then a gate where the cows stood dark in the moonlight close enough to touch, eyeing the pair dully. Adam reached for the latch on the gate and whispered to Leo, "No lock."

He silently turned the latch, and the two slowly pulled the gate open, making a large opening to the lot, a portal from the pile of refuse into the great wide world. The cows could wander into a wide field with no sign of manure, a field with stubble left from some recent harvest.

The boys returned to the truck to watch the exodus, and though sometimes a cow would wander past the opening and look onto the outside world, they always turned to return to the food and the piles of crap.

Adam said, "We better get out of here before we get in trouble. That'd be a great way to start an adventure. They'll probably all come out after we leave – well, some of them."

Leo was downcast as they drove back to the campground, muttering, "Stupid cows."

The next day they started early and rumbled through Bakersfield, starting the lengthy haul up the long rises heading west. By the end of the day, they would climb from almost sea level to 7,000 feet. Because they were loaded up, they could not attack these rises at full speed. As the hill slowed them down, they would go into a lower gear, turn off the AC, and open the windows. Adam would adjust his speed by watching the temperature gauge, slowing to a crawl if it rose too high. It was a hot day for the season and they saw cars on the side with their hoods popped open, steam rising. But they took their time and finally felt cooler air as they gained altitude in Arizona.

The long slow rises caused Adam to reflect on this journey and he remembered the "flow" card he had drawn from the reader. Weren't they in the flow just now? Weren't they going where the Universe would send them?

He remembered reading Huckleberry Finn in a college course, years after he had read it as a child. He remembered coming to the brilliant realization that the story was an allegory and the river a metaphor for life. He remembered the paper he had written discussing how Huck's friend, Tom Sawyer, had lived too long with the Widow Douglas who had combed his hair, put shoes on his feet, and taught him table manners. He had been "civilized", completely immersed in the conventions of polite society and he could not see that it was a constructed reality.

Only Huck still had enough wildness in him to tear off the scratchy collars and venture into the flow of life. To Huck the river was his salvation – to Tom it was just a place to catch fish. Huck had asked his friend to accompany him on a raft down the Mississippi but Tom Sawyer, the all-American hero of his own book, had too much fear to take the chance.

Adam was committed to letting the flow take him where it would, someplace predetermined by a greater force. He swore he had not been too long with "the Widow." He had not forgotten entirely who he really was and what he could be.

The cactus, dust, and yucca gave way to cedar and juniper. It felt good to let the air spin around the cab. Little by little the Ponderosa pines came into view along the interstate – first one or two, then large stands of towering trees spreading their needled hands out wide to bless the land and these two pilgrims.

Adam sought to introduce Leo to the native fauna. "Those are Ponderosa Pine; not as big as Redwoods, but really big trees. And that's about the only tree that grows here except for Aspens. The campground in Flagstaff is a Ponderosa forest."

Leo stared at the welcoming trees and said, "Cool."

Adam felt as if he had come there to receive a gift. He reveled in the anticipation, mixed with fear of the adventure that waited for him – he just needed to open to it. He knew many others could not make this journey even if their world had fallen apart. He held sadness and forgiveness for the ones who could not rise above their hurt, their grief.

He knew that he was grieving too. How could he not? And he knew his healing was just beginning. The work would be grueling but he sensed the outcome would be peace and joy. He certainly was grieving the loss of his marriage – anticipated months of struggle to release this burden.

But, even more, he was grieving the loss of the old man, the old Adam, who must be dissolved to make way for his rebirth, his reimagining. He trusted that Justine would be his guide, but he could not count on that. The messages from her had been cryptic and reserved. She was very encouraging, but he was dismayed that after all their time together, he could not read her better. There were hidden places that he longed to know, to explore. But they belonged to her and she kept them veiled.

Adam had vacationed in this part of Arizona frequently. When Cherie had found the Airstream and imagined her Ralph Lauren guest house, they had spoken of trekking to Sedona and camping by the creek. They had made a trip or two to peer into the Grand Canyon, staying at the Grand Tovar instead of camping.

They had discovered Macy's Coffee House in Flagstaff which served the best cappuccino Adam had ever tasted. The place was filled with the perfect combination of counter culture types and professors and students from the university – a hearty stew of dreadlocks and tweed jackets; he loved it.

Cherie had loved staying at a nice resort in Sedona while he savored most the hikes into the canyons – climbing over fallen rocks, taking in the mystic vista. He felt those transcendent places calling to him now and knew they would somehow figure into his awakening.

THIRTEEN – COMPLETION

The final card for Adam . . . . Because he had lost his strength, his connection to the world of form, the reader turned the card. It showed a pleasant smiling face, slightly Asian – like a Buddha – mostly blue and white, the picture broken into puzzle pieces with the last piece being set in place by, he thought, The Divine. At the bottom of the card was the word: "Completion".

She said, "You will draw this many times before you rest. You do not set the piece in place yourself. And notice the puzzle piece is placed into the center of your forehead, from where you can know without seeing. You will allow your destiny to unfold before you, to take its own shape. Its shape was determined long ago, before you took form, and you cannot make it happen faster – or slower – than intended. Notice this is true of all others and do not begrudge the quicker or the slower yoke they have been given – it is all in Divine Order.

Adam gazed at the card, seeking solace, feeling the final piece was far ahead, beyond his view, beyond his imagining.

Pulling into the western edge of Flagstaff, they rented a space at the Woody Campground, setting up camp in a forest of soaring Ponderosa Pines. Leo kept staring at the summit of the tree tops in awe and wonder. When they were set up, they drove into town and sat down with a big pizza and some Cokes. They wandered around the downtown a little after dinner, but were anxious to return to the campground and the easy comfort of the trailer. They stopped by the campground store on their return to stock up on a few things they needed: some bottled water and a quart of milk for the growing boy.

The store was a simple wood frame building with an old west plank porch out front, sheltered by a metal corrugated roof that protected the patrons from the frequent summer monsoons. Two long benches flanked either side of the porch, inviting customers and visitors to rest a moment, to breathe in the fragrant pine and the fresh washed gravel drive. They chanced upon the nightly gathering of a group of single men who were longer-term tenants of the campground, some retired widowers or divorcés and some construction workers here for the season.

They were full of stories and lies and good humored ribbing – Adam thought, joy. Adam and Leo sat on the edge of the group soaking up the ambiance. Adam had a beer and sometimes joined in the conversation. Leo pulled on a chocolate milk and shyly answered a barrage of curiosity aimed at him.

An old man with a grizzled white beard engaged the shy youngster. "What's your name, son. We don't get too many young folks who want to hang out with this sorry bunch."

He replied weakly, "Name's Leo."

The camper was encouraged. "Hey, Leo the lion. Where you from, son? And who's that fellow you're with?"

"Drove here from Santa Rosa." Leo motioned to Adam. "That's Adam. He's. . . ."

His voice trailed off and Adam spoke up, "I'm his dad. We're on our way to Sedona."

The answer seemed to satisfy the interrogator and to please the lion. Leo stood out in this crowd but that made him a celebrity, not an outsider. It was their little joke – the black kid with the white guy – and it led to endless verbal sparring between them.

At nightfall, a ragged looking man with a ragged small dog walked into the group. He was clearly homeless and smelled of beer. He made his hellos and went into the store to buy dog food for his pet (probably), but nothing for himself. Outside he found a seat, flipped the top of one of the cans and spilled the contents out onto the deck boards. The dog ate ravenously while Adam and Leo looked on. The rest of the group seemed to shun this man, uncomfortable with this outcast among outcasts.

Adam engaged the man a little and learned he was heading to the interstate – hitchhiking east, then south, maybe he'd try to find some family. Adam reached into his pocket looking for a couple dollars and discovered he had only twenties neatly folded. He hesitated; they were on a budget. Then he peeled off a bill, folding it carefully into fourths. When he handed it to the man, he held onto his hand for a moment and fixed onto his eyes. "I want you to go inside right now and buy yourself some food – I'm going to wait. Then, keep the rest for your journey."

He stared intently at the old looking young man, transmitting an unspoken message, a blessing. The man seemed confused for a moment, then accepted the intent. Adam waited until he came back out with some bologna and a loaf of bread. He and Leo said their goodbyes and walked back to the trailer.

On the way, Leo wondered out loud, "Think he'll drink with that?"

Adam responded, "I don't know. You never know what results your actions will produce."

They let the darkness settle over them, thinking there is so much sadness in the world, what can one person do but show a little kindness. It's like tossing a stone into a still pond. Then you sit back and wait for the ripples.

Adam turned the topic a little. "Hope I didn't embarrass you back there. We never talked about what we're supposed to call each other. You didn't mind did you?"

Leo said, "I don't mind. But . . . do you want me to call you . . . dad?"

Adam laughed. "It sounds a little funny doesn't it? Even to me. Let's just see how it goes. A lot of kids call their parents by their first names, don't they? Isn't that hip?"

Leo responded, "Yeah, that's what we are . . . hip."

Adam had something to add. "But just so you know. I am your dad, for better or worse. And that's not going to change."

Leo said, "I know."

In Sedona, Justine had moved her life into a modest stucco house in the middle of town, just a short drive down from the rocky red hills and monuments into a less visible, hidden corner of town. It was cooler here because of the shade cast by sycamores and massive cottonwood trees. If you stopped, you could hear Oak Creek tumbling over rocks just a short walk from her front door. She had a long backyard enclosed by a stucco wall. The owners had planted a grassy lawn in a part of the state that was famous for its xeriscapes and landscaping with cactus and yucca and rocks.

At the back of the lawn, the rough, textured wall provided a support for climbing pink roses and ivy vines. Justine busied herself with pulling weeds from small patches of lettuce, carrots, and beets. There were flowers among the vegetables – orange marigolds... columbine... a fragrant clump of lavender. Her tomato plants had shot up to above her knees, and she had tied them to wooden stakes with green ribbon.

She pushed her bare hands into the warm soil to feel this element that calmed her, that quieted the intensity that pervaded much of her existence here. She had an overwhelming sensation that the Earth was new, just now reborn. And, she was here to help it move into its next undefined and unrestricted imagining.

It was just the dirt in a corner of her garden but when she slid her hand beneath the soil, she was connected to all the earth and all the life it held – everywhere. She remembered the story of the Buddha, who dipped his toe in the stream and knew he was connected to the river that received the stream. He was connected to the ocean that received the river and to all the oceans and far away seas it finally touched. And, he was connected to the source of the tiny stream: the mountain tops capped with snow that melted slowly in the summer sun for no other purpose but to show the Buddha that all things are connected, all things are only one thing.

Justine knew this was the scheduled day for Adam and Leo to arrive. They had decided to start their new life here, she knew, because of her presence. She had promised nothing and she did not know if they would complicate or bless her existence. She was finally in a place that welcomed and nurtured her. She would be happy to bring young Leo into her home – her circle – where she felt he could grow into his strength.

Then there was Adam. He was a joy to her – he was sincere and enthusiastic for his own re-imagining. He was anxious, impatient to be fully awake. He was always trying – not to try. She wondered if their mutual attraction to each other was a help or a hindrance. Wouldn't his transition be smoother if he could focus only on his own journey? She could see his heart, his intention. That was the first quality she had seen in him and she had found it endearing, even as he stumbled over his words on the day they first met in her office.

She sensed that they were near, possibly squinting into the same morning light.

Adam and Leo awoke early to greet the new born day. The sun blessed the tree tops and its light filtered through the fragrant needles to the picnic table where they sipped their respective coffee and orange juice. They had just finished a nice breakfast which Adam had produced on the thirty-year-old

Airstream stovetop, and now they were appreciating the ambiance of the wooded campground.

They planned their descent to Sedona. Leo wanted to go through Oak Creek Canyon, but Adam opted for the longer route down the interstate which would be friendlier for pulling the trailer. He promised Leo they would travel the scenic drive on another day when they would be free to stop and explore.

They would also arrive in Sedona from the south which was a jaw-dropping drive itself.

Adam was brimming with anticipation as they hitched up the trailer and headed onto the interstate down the mountain. They would drop two thousand feet to Sedona.

As they entered the Village of Oak Creek the first rock formations came into view. They passed Bell Rock, Leo staring at the pyramid shape, and continued north toward town. They were greeted around every turn by a fresh view of towering rock shapes, sky a cobalt blue, and the perfect dusting of fluffy white clouds. "This must surely be heaven." Adam thought. "Who ever gets the opportunity to live in a place like this?"

They had a reservation at an RV park, Rancho Sedona, and backed into a gravel pad shadowed by towering sycamores and cottonwood trees. The lowness of the land, the proximity to the creek, and the abundance of shade kept this spot a little cooler than much of the town. The thirty-year-old air conditioner had been fully tested but Adam felt it had had a long eventful life so would one day soon just stop and die. Adam had found directions to Justine's home when he Googled it on his laptop, and she knew their itinerary; she knew they would arrive today.

Adam thought he should not be overly anxious. He would be cool, nonchalant, like "I just happened to be in the neighborhood – thought I'd look you up." Who was he kidding? He had it bad, and felt like a teenager with a crush on the inaccessible cheerleader. He was startled and a little dismayed about these feelings. He thought it must look like silliness to the target of his affections, Justine. He was constantly analyzing his feelings, his intentions. He did not want to approach this woman out of neediness – that thought sickened him.

He knew he could be whole and vital on his own. He knew the work ahead of him – the becoming his true Self – was solitary work. But he would land in the world of form and there would be Leo, his young lion. He knew he had assumed an awesome responsibility for this being – and he knew as well that Leo would lift him, would inspire him, would give light to his path. He could not say if he would land also next to Justine. The future was a dense fog, he could make out no forms or figures. It did not exist, and this thought gave him heart. He could not see her from his tidy spot in the RV park, but he knew she was here, now, nearby, almost close enough to touch.

In his daydreaming, he reached out his hand before him, clutching air. Leo walked around the corner of the trailer. Seeing his guardian with that now familiar faraway look, he just shook his head and muttered, "Kids."

It was early evening by the time the trailer was unhitched and hooked up to power, water, and sewer. When they were sure it was all set and locked up securely, they climbed into the pickup, Google map in hand. Leo was also anxious to see his friend and counsel and hoped she would be home. Off of Brewer Road, they took the side road down again toward the creek. They found the house at the end of the drive and parked the truck.

No one answered their knocks so they looked into the long backyard surrounded by an adobe wall. Past the gate, Adam saw her working in the garden, head and face covered by a wide straw hat, dressed down in jeans and a white linen shirt. Even cloaked, she was a vision. Adam would have stood there for days, just gazing, but Leo yelled, "Justine!"

She turned, unsurprised, and graced them with a smile. They opened the gate and walked into the yard, she glided forward to meet them. Leo ran ahead into her outstretched arms – was this his family now? Adam had to wait his turn and she eventually walked into his arms. He bent to kiss her but she turned her head and focused back on Leo, gathering all the news. She led them to her patio where the table was already set with three plates, glasses, and silver ware.

Adam asked, "Are you expecting company?"

She smiled and said, "Yes."

She poured them lemonade and went into the house to bring out a modest dinner of salad and some kind of warm grain with veggies, beans, and corn. Very healthy, Adam thought and Leo feared.

They sat like a family, talking and laughing. Leo related the stories of the road, their continuing journey into deeper knowing, compassion, and understanding. Justine hung on every word, focusing on Leo but keeping Adam in her field of vision.

Adam rested there, like he was finally home. Through a forest of cottonwoods behind her back fence, he could see a vast wall of orange rock that grew brighter and more golden as the sun reached for the western horizon. Ruby-throated hummingbirds vibrated around two feeders on the patio, rocketing in for the nectar, then disappearing with a blur and the sound of air against tiny rapid feathers.

Small, brownish doves paired up on the ridge of the garden shed, cooing softly to each other, suggesting intimacy or something deeper. Leo and Justine finally took a breath and noticed his quietness. He raised his hands, palms up, and said, "What?"

Leo tried to encourage him. "Nothing, man. Just . . . you know . . . social skills."

Justine defended. "It's okay, Adam." Then to Leo, "Sometimes, saying nothing can be very profound. Besides, we haven't given him much of a chance."

The time seemed short, and the shadows thrown by the trees had lengthened. When the time was ready Justine rose and sent them home. Adam caught a moment alone with her as they were leaving.

"It's just so great to see you . . . you can't know what it means to me. I thought we'd have more time alone, but really,

I don't care. I'm happy just to be in the same space with you, just to breathe the same air."

Justine gave him the slightest smile. "That worries me a little."

He protested, "But, why?"

"It's the intensity – you have to let that wane. Be careful about the fantasy you're creating. Look inside. Who is doing this? What part of you?"

Adam was distraught. "I'm so confused and scattered. I know that. I don't blame you for holding back. I don't know what in the hell I'm doing – I know that too. Won't you just tell me how to do this?"

"It's a new world now, and you have just moved into the center of it. This place requires conscious relationships – we cannot repeat anything that resembles the patterns of the past."

Adam was sure she understood and could just tell him if she wanted to. He felt like she had the key but held back so he would learn the lesson on his own. He did not realize that she was also just feeling her way into new realms, willing to let it be.

The next day Justine agreed to meet Adam at a coffee shop in town. Leo agreed to stay behind at the campground; he understood. Before Adam left, the two settled into the comfortable camp chairs around their collapsible poly table. Leo munched on breakfast cereal while Adam sipped his first cup of coffee and gazed up at the canopy of green spread by the enormous grove of sycamores. He was settling into a habit of quiet introspection and the peace and the energy of the place made this quite inviting.

Although he was not seeking clarity, although he had simply settled into acceptance and surrender, an understanding settled over him like a low cloud. The Tower Card was a blessing, a gift. This was simple grace: what he could not do for himself, the Universe had intervened to accomplish. It was not in him to leave his wife, to leave everything he knew, to take the enormous risk of starting his own life over, so the Universe came to rip all that from his grip. He was overwhelmed with a deep sense of gratitude for the miraculous series of events that had changed his life irreversibly and forever.

He had a sudden welling of emotion with this understanding. We only imagine that we love and desire these things that keep us from realizing our potential, our highest expression. For Adam they were his marriage, his house, his job, his sense of belonging and comfortable living in a community that seemed to provide acceptance and support, even Justine.

Things had to become uncomfortable in order for him to finally make a move. He knew that we all have these Tower Card moments – they do not feel kind, they do not feel like God – but they are a rare and powerful expression of the Divine.

Adam saw now, it was not about being unhappy with his circumstances. Sometimes the Tower Card is drawn when all seems well. Sometimes we are blinded by our beliefs or the fantasies we have imagined, and nothing but a smack in the face or a kick in the ass will give us the necessary push to get us up and to get to get us on. We could imagine that the Universe is cold and unfeeling for violently stripping us of what might be our deepest desire, but that would only happen when that desire is hiding the truth from our eyes.

Adam eased into some understanding about the pitfall of having too much desire for the things of the world, and wondered if his desire for Justine might be just another trap, set by the surface mind. He wondered if he was particularly susceptible to falling back to sleep, to creating fantastical places to rest that shrouded his awareness. Was it just him or was this the great disease that plagued the human race? He was not ready for this much truth, so he quickly wiped it from his wakefulness.

Leo broke the trance, saying, "Don't you have a date?"

Adam regained his footing. "You sure you're okay here by yourself?

"Look around. What could I get into? I'll just take a walk; check out the place. You sure you're okay without a wing-man?"

"I am sure of nothing. But some things you have to do alone."

Leo wanted to be encouraging. He said, "Be courageous."

"Thanks."

"What I really mean is . . . don't blow it."

"Now that makes me feel a lot better."

Adam climbed into the pickup and left the campground, with Leo looking after the disappearing Chevy, silently cheering him on. Adam drove the pickup through town, gaping at the red rock formations, conscious that he did not want to look like a tourist. This was complicated by the fact he had California license plates, which he thought put a bulls-eye on his behind. He made a mental note to visit the Arizona DMV as soon as possible.

He navigated the new round-a-bouts deftly, not holding up traffic, sliding around the cars from Iowa full of folks with wide eyes and worried faces. He found Justine's favorite coffee house in an indescript strip mall, fairly hidden from potential customers. Guess you just had to know – he knew.

As usual, Adam found a table and got himself a cappuccino. The Java Love coffee house was not fancy. It held a variety of mismatched tables and chairs bunched closely together. The place felt good, brimming with happy sippers: folks on laptops showing each other their recent finds, local art on the wall. A bulletin board held fliers for live music events, shamanic healers, and spirituality themed cruises. He felt happy here, some inexplicable happiness.

Adam told himself, this is the heart of the town. Strangers smiled at him and said hello, like they already knew him – maybe they did. At the table next to him three guys were buzzing with excitement about some recent adventure. He could not help overhearing them talk about laying down tracks. They were working on some studio recording project, each of them contributing a different part of the music. Adam realized he was staring intently at the center of their conversation when one of them – a man of similar years, dark hair, and a goatee – engaged him. "I'm Simon – I don't think I've seen you in here before."

Adam was embarrassed for being caught staring. "No, I'm new in town. I couldn't help listening to you guys talking about your music."

Simon was friendly. "Are you a musician?"

Adam had to think before responding. "Yes. Yes, I am. I play guitar and write some songs. My son plays percussion."

Simon introduced the other guys around the table and they bantered about instruments and music styles and over this influence and that. Simon pulled out a business card and wrote an address at the bottom.

"Join us at the studio tomorrow. Bring your kid. We've got a drummer but we could use some more percussion. You . . . I don't know. Let's just see how it goes. What does your son play?"

"It's a box drum . . . called a cajon."

Simon was genuinely interested. "Really? I've seen those . . . it might be a good sound for our project. Where'd you get it?"

Adam answered, "We made it."

"No kidding? Could you make another one?"

"Yeah, I guess."

Simon and his crew were heading out but he scribbled something onto his business card and handed it to Adam. "Stop by around two. Address is on the card. Should be fun."

Adam took the card and studied it. "I'm there."

There was something moving inside of him – it was palpable. He closed his eyes and felt it fill him up. He flashed on the Fool Card and thought about unlimited potential. He suddenly remembered why he was here today and pulled his thoughts back to the present moment. He felt like he needed to prepare himself for this meeting and wished he had written down some talking points.

He yearned for her, this Justine. He wanted this woman but he had decided that having her could not – would not – be his objective. In his heart, and he would follow that, he just wanted to know her, wanted to learn from her without emptying her. He never knew it was possible to love someone so deeply and still not have the need to hold onto them.

Holding on to her was restricting, limiting, even controlling. Of course, for him it was still a stretch. He was not free from all the old patterns; the temptation to move back into neediness and jealousy. This was something exquisitely beautiful and he had to approach it with grace, with reverence, with courage. He swore he would not repeat the errors, the patterns of the past.

She came in from the glaring, blessing, light. She wore a long linen dress, a cloak of deepest blue pulled around her. She was the ocean and the sky; the mysteries swirled around her head.

Adam knew somehow he would have to make her human in his mind; he could not keep up the fantasy. But, he felt he saw her truer than anybody else, deeper, more complete.

He felt he saw her as she had been created: a perfect, flawless being.

Something small and quiet spoke within him. One day soon, in its own time, he would step off this section of the trail and onto one that stretched into the great unknown, the unnamed. He would emerge onto the other side of this learning and he would miss the fantasy.

As usual, she got her tea and settled in across from him. He could not contain his boyish cheerfulness and his face could not break from smiling. She sat, seeming comfortable in her skin and waited to look at him, playing with her tea. He lingered, anxious for her to surface. It was a spectacular wait – like watching the sun rise and spread its blessed light across the land. Then, without warning – the raised head – a toothy smile, and the eyes that still melted something at his core. He could not remember any of his good intentions.

He was speechless, so she started, "How's Leo?"

"He's great. He seems completely at home with being adrift. Teaching me how to be."

"What about Cherie? How did that go?"

Adam was surprised about her raising this topic, but he answered truthfully. "That was hard. I guess I thought I'd just drive away."

"It's a big chunk of your life. You'll have to grieve."

"Feels like I've been grieving for years. I want to be done with that."

"I understand that's what you want. But, you're not finished. Sorry, it's a process."

He said, "I feel some healing around the whole thing. It could have been nasty, and it really wasn't. It might sound funny, but I have a new appreciation for her."

"That's very healthy. She's been important for your development – critical even. You would not be here without her. And you brought her into your awareness. Whatever she gave you – good or bad – you attracted it to yourself for a reason. She's a gift."

Adam saw an opening, "Just like I've attracted you to me now."

Justine spoke slowly and carefully, "Okay."

They didn't speak for a minute, then Adam asked, "So what about this?" He motioned to the space between them. "What about this unspoken, sacred, undefined thing? Any breakthroughs there?"

Justine paused a moment and smiled broadly. "Just to let it be."

Adam slid his hand toward her, palm up, across the table at Java Love, and she covered it with her own.

EPILOGUE

Back at the towering live oak in the middle of the town plaza, the sky was just beginning to lose power. The sun, moving lower to the western horizon, was throwing beams of golden light onto the farmer's market, the sidewalks, and the deep blue cloak of the Tarot reader. She turned over the top card for herself. It read "Ordinariness". This gave her ease. It would be so until she was again called into service.

She calmly pulled the cards together into a neat pile and placed them into a small wooden box just big enough to hold them. The reader gathered all her things in a woven bag and walked from the tree toward the rows of tables selling strawberries and spring onions. She was facing into the setting sun and she allowed the hood to fall absently onto her back. She emerged brilliant and angelic into the light.

There was a portly farmer selling cherry tomatoes to a pretty blond. He caught just a flash of blue and gold as the reader sauntered past. He looked around to see if anyone else had noticed, and asked Cherie, "What was that?"

The reader took two more steps, and then she had vanished completely.

Sedona worked its magic on Adam and Leo as they humbly took their places in this remarkable setting. On his first Saturday in town, Justine brought Adam with her to what she called a "gratitude circle". They sat on chairs in a wide arc and everyone spoke to something they were thankful for;

nothing else was permitted. It was easy for Adam; he was grateful for being there and for sharing a common space with Justine. This ritual became a weekly event for him and he was overwhelmed by the feeling of love and acceptance he felt there.

The invitation to jam with Simon and the other musicians turned into another weekly ritual. Leo took to making music with this group like he was a consummate professional. It was always the highlight of their week, and they would anticipate it like children waiting for Christmas morning. Adam networked with the musicians and found his entry into the world of musicianship in Sedona. He soon discovered that there was no music store in the town; no place to buy a guitar, or sheet music, or even reeds for a high school student's clarinet.

With his savings, he leased an empty storefront in Uptown and filled it with stringed instruments and hand drums which turned out to be very popular in Sedona. Leo happily went to work as a salesman when he wasn't in school. Adam remembered Bud's prophetic words about the cajon, and he started building some in the shop behind the music store. He was surprised to see the first one he set out sell within days.

When he put up a site on the internet, he received more orders than he could fill. Adam got a hold of his old employee, Antonio, in Santa Rosa and together they made plans for him to move out with his wife and two kids. Antonio would work in the shop full time, building the box drums, feeding the insatiable demand that continued to pour in from the internet. Adam and Leo reluctantly moved out of the Airstream into a little house with a view of towering rock formations and the infinite cobalt sky.

Whenever he could, Adam hiked down to a hidden formation of slide rock in the magical and healing Oak Creek. He would plunge his bare feet into the everlasting water and be reminded to resist the impulse to put down roots. Now was the time to be available and he imagined setting into the flow on a raft that would surely bring him to his truth.

When a customer walked into the shop looking for a guitar like the professionals used, Leo pulled one off the wall and proudly handed it over. "It's a Taylor . . . one of the best. Same one that Tony Mazzella plays."

The customer fingered the fret board and studied the workmanship, just as Adam walked out of the back room holding a shiny mahogany cajon. He said, "Look at this one, Leo. It's a beauty. Already sold, but I'm going to display it until the guy comes in to pick it up."

Antonio stood in the doorway of the shop appreciating the praise for his workmanship. Leo said, "Good work Antonio. You're a master."

Adam reminded his young master salesman, "Don't forget . . . we've got practice tonight."

A bell jangled when Justine entered the store. Adam was glad to see her and greeted her with a kiss to the cheek. He asked, "You here to see me?"

"Sorry, no – I'm here to see Leo." Then she focused on Leo. "I was just in the neighborhood . . . a friendly reminder. . . ."

Leo was ready. "I know . . . noon tomorrow . . . I'll be there. Am I going to get some lunch?"

"Absolutely."

"Any chance of getting some meat?"

Justine looked over her glasses at him. "Don't push it." Then she made her apologies, "I've got to run now . . . I'll see you all later."

Justine made a point of talking to Adam before she left. "So how's business? You guys making a go of it?"

Adam answered, "We've had some challenges. But it's been one amazing day after another. I just hired a new guy to help Antonio build the cajons. We're selling the drums on our website faster than we can make them."

"I'm so happy for you. You look good."

"Thanks, I just never had the courage to dream this big. By the way, you look pretty good yourself."

Leo, who had been listening in, rolled his eyes. Justine kissed Adam on the cheek and headed for the door. She said, "Call me . . . we'll do coffee."

Adam saw her to the door. As she made her way down the sidewalk he looked after her with appreciation and a little bit of desire. He went back to the sales counter with a big smile.

Leo questioned him, "What are you thinking?"

He said, "I'm not thinking nothing."

"Right."

A few minutes later a woman walked in the front door and Leo greeted her. She was pretty with dark hair, forty-something, with pale skin and red lips. "Hey Joy, good to see you. You here for that guy?" He pointed his thumb at Adam who was busy with something at the cash register.

She answered, "We're going to lunch . . . if he can tear himself away."

Leo yelled over his shoulder to the boss, "Adam, your lunch is here!" Then quieter to Joy, "Hey, if he's too busy, I'll buy you a taco."

Adam hurried to intervene, "I'm ready." He kissed Joy on the lips and they headed out the door, giving Leo one last bit of direction, "Okay, son – you're in charge."

Leo said, "Scary."

Adam and Joy left the music store arm in arm in search of a cozy place to sit and eat and visit. Leo watched them walk away, and then he dug his hand into his jeans pocket and pulled out the piece of blue sea-glass. He looked into the jewel for a long while, like he was retrieving a message that was hidden there, and then he gazed dreamily out the store window to the red rocks and the impossibly blue sky.

That night, Adam introduced the band to the blues piece he had written so long ago and which he and Leo and Bud had mastered in the tattered garage studio. Leo sat on his box drum and pretended to tune it, impatient for launching into the music. Adam started the tune, picking out the melody with Leo right on his heels, expertly sounding out a soft and soulful rhythm on the cajon. Another percussionist on a drum set followed Leo's lead. Simon was on the bass this time, and he picked up the back beat. The keyboards and rhythm guitar joined them to make a perfectly joyous sound.

The father and the son locked eyes from across the room, and they spoke to each other without words, each immersed in the present sacred moment.

THE END

Acknowledgements

Thank you to the Gratitude Circle at Unity of Sedona,
Suzie who saw me through the dark days, my family –
brothers, nieces and nephews, and the sisters who raised me,
Mark Jackson Pope in a baseball cap, Tricia and Andy,
Tom Bird my writing coach, Joyce Kaye my editor,
the Osho Zen Tarot and Osho International, Roger Wyer,
Adyashanti, Rasha, Eckhart, Erich Fromm, Mark Twain,
William Pete Kelley, Dr. Stewart Ryder, A Course in Miracles,
The Sedona Writers Group, The Earth School for Souls,
Penny and Carol, Anthony Mazzella, Eric Zang,
and The Java Love Coffee House.

About the Author

John Berry Deakyne is a writer, poet and spiritual teacher living in Sedona, Arizona. He weaves profound spiritual teaching into his stories of everyday folks caught in extraordinary circumstances. He is also the author of *The Devil Card – The Redemption of Lucifer* which is the second book in his *Tarot Series.*

He teaches *The Earth School for Souls,* where "we all work to step through the darkness of our individual stories into the light of living in the Truth of our Being."

John's popular blog is called *"on the road to find out"* and it chronicles his own journey of awakening:

http://sedonawordsmith.blogspot.com

The author may be contacted at:

Sedona Wordsmith

PO Box 1726

Sedona, Arizona 86339.

Website: http://www.sedonawordsmith.com